Rhea melted in Jamie's arms, hanging on to his shoulders for support. But for his arms which had curved around her slim waist, she would have sunk to the floor, her legs having gone weak and rubbery. She opened her lips to let his tongue in and felt her heart hammer against her chest as he explored her mouth thoroughly, making sounds of appreciation in his throat which aroused her to fever pitch.

It was a while before they came up for air and Rhea buried her face on his chest. So that's how a kiss felt! It was explosive, mind blowing! She took deep breaths to calm her heart but it simply refused to listen.

But Rhea being Rhea, she was keen to check out Jamie's mouth, the same way he had explored hers. Raising her head from his chest, she locked her arms around his neck, pulling his head down. She ran a damp tongue over the seam of his lips, seeking entry.

ABOUT THE AUTHOR

Sundari Venkatraman is an Indie Author who has 60 books to her credit. These books have consistently featured in the Top 100 Bestseller Lists on Amazon India, Amazon USA, Amazon UK, Amazon Canada and Amazon Australia in both romance as well as Asian Drama categories. Her latest hot romances have all been on #1 Bestseller slot in Amazon India for over a month.

ROSE GARDEN INTERNATIONAL is the second of The Bansal Legacy trilogy which are novels set in the background of 5-star hotels. This kindle book remained in #1 Bestseller position on Amazon India for two whole months in the Contemporary Romance and Asian Drama categories.

Even as a child, Sundari absolutely loved the 'lived happily ever after' syndrome and she grew up on a steady diet of fairy tales, Phantom comics and Mandrake comics. It was always about good triumphing over evil and a happy ending after the protagonists surmounted all unexpected obstacles.

Once she entered her teens, Sundari switched her loyalties from fairy tales to Mills & Boon. While she loved reading both of these, she kept visualising what would have happened if there were similar situations happening in India; to local heroes and heroines. And of course, the joy of vanquishing the ubiquitous evil villains! Her imagination soared and she happily ensconced herself in a rosy romantic cocoon for many years.

Then came the writing—a true bolt from the blue! And Sundari Venkatraman has never looked back.

Books by Sundari Venkatraman

Standalone novels
The Malhotra Bride
Meghna
The Madras Affair
An Autograph for Anjali
Twin Torment
Finding Anya
Mr. Perfect
Man Friday
Her Prince Charming
Love in Agartha
Arjun's Penance
The Floundering Author
Once Bitten Twice Lucky
Ryan Finds a Bride
Tinder Loving Care
Shaan Gets Hitched
For Better or For Worse
Heartthrob
Call of the Heart

Collection of shorts
Matches Made in Heaven
Tales of Sunshine

The Groom Series Trilogy
#1 Groomnapped
#2 Gobsmacked
#3 Grounded

Dashavatar (Indian Mythology)
MATSYA: The First Avatar
KURMA: The Second Avatar
VARAHA: The Third Avatar
NARASIMHA: The Fourth Avatar
VAMANA: The Fifth Avatar
PARASHURAMA: The Sixth Avatar

The Writer's Toolkit (Non-fiction)
Publishing Your Book on Amazon KDP

Marriages Made in India Series
#1 The Runaway Bridegroom
#2 Her Smitten Husband
#3 His Drunken Wife
#4 Her Secret Husband
#5 The Casanova's Wife
#6 Her Bohemian Husband

The Bansal Legacy Trilogy
#1 Simha International
#2 Rose Garden International
#3 Maharaja International

Written in the Stars Series
#1 Scorpio Superstar
#2 Leo's Desire
#3 Taurus Temptation
#4 Virgo's Krush

The Thakore Royals Trilogy
#1 The Marriage Predicament
#2 Tied in Knots
#3 The Wooing of the Shrew

Romantic Shorts
#1 *Chahti Hoon Tumhe*
#2 Beauty is but Skin Deep
#3 Madeinheaven.com
#4 An Arranged Match
#5 The Reluctant Bride
#6 *Shweta ka Swayamvar*
#7 Papa's Girl
#8 Red Rose Dating Agency
#9 Rahat Mili
#10 Reema's Matchmakers
#11 The Matchmaker's Dream

The Princess Series (Historical Romance)
#1 The Passionate Princess
#2 The Rebel Princess

THE BANSAL LEGACY
BOOK #2

ROSE GARDEN
INTERNATIONAL

SUNDARI VENKATRAMAN

FLAMING SUN

Notion Press Media Pvt Ltd

No. 50, Chettiyar Agaram Main Road,
Vanagaram, Chennai, Tamil Nadu – 600 095

First Published by Flaming Sun 2017
Printed & Distribution by Notion Press
Copyright © Sundari Venkatraman 2022
All Rights Reserved.

ISBN 979-8-88749-990-1

Cover design by: Unaiza Merchant
Beta read by: Rubina Ramesh
Edited & marketed by: The Book Club

DEDICATION

This special March birthday edition is for my sister Lakshmi. Despite the age gap between us, she's my best friend. While being the youngest of us five sisters, Lakshmi also happens to be the wisest. Love you Lak!

"The great advantage of a hotel is that it is a refuge from home life"

– George Bernard Shaw

ACKNOWLEDGEMENT

I would like to thank the following people for all their help while I did the research for *The Bansal Legacy* series. (This was sometime in the year 2005)

Mr Suresh Shetty, Director, Hotel Ashray International, Sion

Mr Vithal Kamat, Chairman and General Manager, The Orchid, Vile Parle

The names and designations below are from 2005 when I did my research. These people must have moved on to bigger positions by now, I am sure:

- Ms Rajul Semal, Environment Executive, The Orchid
- Mr Vikas Kumar, Management Trainee, The Orchid
- Mr Sachin Bhosle, Shift Engineer, The Orchid
- Ms Aparna Desai, Housekeeping, The Orchid
- Mr J. B. Singh, Senior Executive, Stores, The Orchid
- Mr Shailesh, Asst. EDP Manager, The Orchid
- Mr Gautam, Jr. Sous Chef, The Orchid

AUTHOR'S NOTE

Ooty is a hill station in Tamil Nadu, South India and is at 7350 feet above sea level. The language spoken is Tamil. It was during a family trip there when I realised that a large number of North Indians were settled in the city, running many business establishments. Which was the reason why my heroine, Rhea Bansal, who is from Maharashtra, decides to set up her 5-star property in Ooty.

Another thing I would like to mention here is, the Tamil people rarely have surnames. Shiva or Kandasamy or Vadivel or Elango are just that, without surnames; while some of them like Velusamy Nadar use their caste name as surname. But Ajit Parmar and Rhea Bansal herself, who are from the Northern states of India, do have surnames.

I have used a few Tamil and Hindi phrases in the dialogues. Footnotes tend to distract the reader. But rest easy that the meanings have been made clear in subsequent dialogues. I don't want the readers to miss the meaning under any circumstance.

J amie Scott stood at the veranda railing, staring at the sunset without really seeing it. His sculpted body, clad only in a pair of brief shorts, gleamed in the red light of the setting sun. He lifted the can of chilled beer to take a deep swig, lost in his own world. It wasn't as if Jamie didn't like crowds. But he was undergoing a strange restlessness; a call of the soul is how the aborigines would term it.

The houseful of guests at his parents' home in Brisbane failed to garner his attention. All of Jamie's three brothers were busy tending to the steaks cooking on the barbeque while his sisters-in-law were watching the kids—five at the last count—ranging from age one to seven.

Cynthia Way, the daughter of his parents' closest neighbour, walked towards the veranda from the garden where most of the guests were sprawled on the grass in the briefest of attires. She couldn't help but admire Jamie's Greek God looks as the sunlight seemed to set fire to his dark blond hair, forming a halo of sorts. The fuzz on his face was at least a week old and made his face glow all the more.

"Hey," she called out to him with a wide smile, her blue eyes leisurely studying his delectable body. Cynthia was a beauty herself; her golden curls, stormy blue eyes and pearly skin covering a shapely body attracting men by the hordes. But the one man she was interested in, Jamie, didn't seem to even be aware of her existence.

Jamie turned left to see Cynthia walking towards him. He smiled automatically, drawing her attention to the laughter creases on his cheeks, his jade green eyes crinkling as the sun's rays hit them directly. "Hey yourself!"

She went to stand next to him, hooking her arm in the crook of his elbow, taking a deep breath to inhale his all-male scent. Her bare leg quivered as it came in contact with his muscular one. She wore brief shorts and a bikini top, which were perfect for the November weather.

"How long do you plan to stay?" she asked. Jamie's visits to his parents were all too brief for her liking. While all his brothers were based in Brisbane, not far from their parents, Jamie chose to live in Alice Springs in the Northern Territory.

Jamie shrugged, his muscles rippling, drawing Cynthia's eyes to his wide chest. She was having trouble with her breathing as her hands itched to touch the springy curls spread liberally there. "I'm leaving the day after tomorrow. Give me a sec. Lemme get rid of this can and I'll join you at the barbeque." Jamie made an about turn to walk into the house to throw the can in the dustbin. Cynthia waited for him right there on the veranda where he had left her. He was only too aware of her interest as she had made it obvious from the time she turned sixteen. But as for him, he never could see her as a girlfriend.

Jamie hooked his arm into Cynthia's and walked along with her towards the crowded garden, refusing to spend time alone with her, much to her disappointment. Once they reached the garden, there were too many people who were ready to claim his attention, not least of all his three nieces and two nephews.

Jamie loved his parents, brothers and their brats. But while he liked being part of his big family, he felt on pins and needles after a couple of days, longing for the solitude of his bachelor pad in Alice Springs.

The banter claimed his attention yet again and Jamie chatted with one and all into the wee hours of the night; he ate, drank and made merry, even while his soul was not really in it.

2

It was barely five in the morning when Rhea Bansal left her home for work as the managing director of Rose Garden International in Ooty. It was just a five-minute walk from her cosy cottage to the compound of the 5-star hotel, a small picket gate connecting the two properties. A horse whinnied in greeting towards her left. She would make time to ride Gulliver, her stallion, sometime in the afternoon. Rhea blew Gulliver a kiss as she walked on to the brilliant white main building which was two stories high. It was built like a mini castle, with a clock tower in the middle, flanked by two smaller towers on either side.

Rhea entered the hotel through the double doors which were made of glass and wood. The doorman, Karan, enthusiastically wished her a 'good morning'. Rhea waved at him fleetingly as she walked into the main hall.

"Good morning, ma'am," greeted Shiva, the front office manager, covering his mouth when a yawn took him by surprise. He couldn't help but notice the frown on his boss's smooth forehead.

"Hello Shiva," greeted Rhea, without a smile on her face. "How was your night? Busy?" There were going to be at least three sets of people checking in late last night.

"Yes, ma'am," said Shiva, rubbing his hands together surreptitiously, hoping to keep sleep away for at least another hour. The night had been hectic. The foreign guests had wanted proper dinner and not just sandwiches from Bugatti, the 24-hour coffee shop. Luckily, Junior Chef Pandian was obliging enough to rustle up a meal at 3 am. Better yet, the guests had been extremely happy with the food and the service at Gold Strike, the restaurant which served Chettinadu cuisine. It was barely half an hour ago when they finally settled in their cottages.

Rhea nodded. "You go on and get a few hours of sleep. I'll man the desk until the others come in."

Shiva looked at his boss. All the staff knew she had a heart of gold, though she rarely smiled. Rhea Bansal appeared to be on pins most of the time, her barks worse than her bite. He squashed the pity which sprung within him for the hardworking young woman. She would probably bite his head off if he showed even a teeny bit of commiseration.

Shiva had been with the hotel from the time Rose Garden International had thrown open its doors to the public. Which had been a little more than three years ago. In such a short span of time, the hotel had become extremely popular with both Indian as well as foreign guests. Shiva had come across the job opening in Rose Garden International soon after he completed fifteen years of experience in the hotel industry holding multiple jobs across the country. He had grabbed the chance to apply for the manager's position in this new 5-star which was to open in his home town of Ooty. His family had been even more thrilled than he was when he got the appointment.

Shiva lifted a hand in her direction and loped off towards the side door, glad of his black jacket as a cold breeze blew from the Emerald Lake which wasn't too far away. In fact, the hotel was built on the surrounding hilly region and looked down upon the serene green waters of the lake. He jogged across the garden which flourished with roses, waving to the two gardeners who were working diligently, one mowing the grass while the other pruned the dead flowers. He reached the car park which was separated from the hotel compound by another picket fence, on the side opposite to the managing director's house. Getting into his car, Shiva drove away to his home with a smile on his face, glad that his shift was going to change from the next day. He would get more time to spend with his wife of two years.

Rhea sat at the reception, sipping from a cup of coffee, running through the entries on the computer, a small smile of satisfaction on her lips. The hotel was full—all hundred cottages occupied. Moreover, the bookings continued till the end of the month. She had been lucky that way, her hotel being almost full whether it was the tourist season or otherwise.

The day staff began to trickle in, one by one, just before the grandfather clock in one corner of the reception hall struck six. All the men and women—there were eight of them—greeted her enthusiastically, with broad smiles. Rhea nodded diligently to each one of them in acknowledgement. The hotel ran like clockwork, its three-hundred-plus employees doing more than what they had signed up for. Attrition was almost nil, while everyone was so happy with their jobs that they rarely took an unscheduled off. Actually, the HR needed to shoo people off for regular breaks which were due to them.

Shouldn't Rhea be happy?

Setting up the hotel had been a challenge. She had been absolutely excited, working in an altogether new environment. Growing up in Mahabaleshwar along with two brothers, one older and one younger, Rhea had enjoyed helping her parents run their family hotel, Bansal Resort.

The three children had decided to carry forward the Bansal legacy by becoming hoteliers themselves. Her elder brother, Rohit Bansal, ran Simha International in Mumbai. Being the eldest, he had been clear that he didn't want to live too far away from their parents. And it had been a year and a half since her young brother Ritvik set up Maharaja International in Udaipur.

Rhea had fallen in love with Ooty during a family holiday some years ago. It so reminded her of the hilly region of Mahabaleshwar. When she found out that a lot of people from North India had made their home in Ooty, Rhea had decided to do the same. And that's how she had got around to setting up Rose Garden

International here. The lake view was a bonus, the surrounding greenery giving the place a tranquil atmosphere.

She purchased the original two-storied structure which stood along with its Dower House—the cottage she lived in— on a huge plot and converted it into the main reception and offices for her hotel. The buildings were obviously from the British era, the structures typical of a small English mansion and its Dower House. She had done her best to retain the original structure which was breathtakingly beautiful, not keen to spoil it with something too modern. Equally interested in retaining the unspoilt atmosphere, she had decided against building tall structures and had gone ahead to build separate cottages on the surrounding land for the guests.

There was also another reason for it. She had modelled her hotel on Bansal Resort, the family hotel in Mahabaleshwar, which also consisted of a batch of independent cottages for the guests.

The variety of roses in Ooty was a major source of inspiration, and Rhea had followed the rose theme for the restaurants and other facilities in the hotel, beginning with the name of the hotel itself.

Rhea had put her heart into hiring the staff, gently refusing help from her brothers. It was, after all, her project and she wanted complete control. Both Rohit and Ritvik knew her too well, refraining from giving free advice after offering just the once. But that hadn't stopped Rohit from visiting the hotel from time to time, checking if things were going well.

Rhea couldn't stop the small smile which sprung to her lips when she thought of her older brother. She had been staring out of her office cabin's window, watching the mist swirling around the guest cottages, her breakfast of a plate of *idli-vadai* with *chutney* and *sambar* lying half-eaten on her desk. Rohit was an adorable brother, who was a rock she could lean on. There were times when she missed her family terribly. But then they did get together as often as they could. Rhea pushed away her plate, the meal unfinished, getting up to walk around her cabin restlessly.

What was she missing? A strange restlessness appeared to have seeped into her mind. Little did Rhea know that Providence was sending an answer to her question the very same week!

J amie used the three-hour flight to Alice Springs to watch a film, having only a bottle of water on his way as he had already eaten breakfast at the Brisbane airport.

As soon as he was out of the airport, Jamie walked swiftly to the airport's parking lot, happy to be back in his space. Getting on his motorcycle which had been parked at the Alice Springs airport, Jamie donned a safety helmet on his head before zipping off to his home which was barely a twenty-minute ride. Stopping outside the gate as he opened it electronically, Jamie glanced with joy at the low-slung building which was his very own. It was a self-contained home with two bedrooms, a large living room, an office space, a sunny kitchen and a work area which consisted of a double sink and a washing machine. The house had even come with its own swimming pool in the backyard—tailor-made for Jamie.

Parking his bike in the front, Jamie took his backpack and went into the coolness of his home, a smile on his face. It was good to be back.

Pulling off his clothes even as he opened the fridge to pick up a can of beer, Jamie stepped out of his back door in his briefs, looking at the pool with pleasure. A neighbour had ensured that the pool was clean and filled with fresh water.

Placing the beer can on the ground next to the pool, Jamie stepped into the cool water and grabbed his beer. He floated on his back, too lazy to swim, sipping from the can. Bliss! Was he glad to be home!

A couple of hours later, having had a sandwich from some cold cuts and fresh bread, he settled down in his office space. Jamie was an interior designer and worked by himself. The two projects which he had completed recently had been humongous successes. Both his clients were happy with his work and had offered to place more his way. As he dithered between three upcoming projects—one was a hotel while the other two were corporate offices—Jamie wasn't sure which one he wanted to take up first. He would rather focus on one and get the designs approved before checking out the next. Jamie liked to be hands-on for all his projects, extremely particular that the specified quality was met with. If two projects ran simultaneously at all, he reached out to sub-contractors only during the execution stages, while he continued to supervise them meticulously.

But no, he didn't plan to take up anything for at least another week. There was something else which needed his attention first. Jamie pulled open the last drawer of his desk and removed some old diaries of his grandmother's which he treasured there. Barbara

Scott had died when Jamie was about ten years old. While she had loved all her four grandsons, Jamie had been her favourite.

"Granny, tell me that story, about the hill station you went to." Jamie had been six when he asked her to narrate her experience at Ooty, a hill station in South India. Little Jamie sat on his grandmother's lap, fascinated by the joy which lit up her softly lined face when she spoke about her two-year stay there before she moved to Australia with his grandfather.

Barbara had laughed gently, stroking Jamie's golden head. He obviously never tired of hearing her talk about Ooty. She must have told him the story at least a dozen times. "It was the most beautiful, lush green landscape which I've ever seen in my life. It shone like a jewel in the morning dew. The winters were cool, reminiscent of my home in Liverpool. Your granddad and I used to go riding for hours..."

While Barbara had spent only a few months over two years of her life in Ooty, the place had left a powerful impact on her. So much so, she had inadvertently passed the impression on to her youngest grandson. Jamie had always wanted to go to Ooty.

He flipped open her diary which was from the year 1944...

October 21, 1944
Dear Diary,
Jason took me on the toy train today, all the way from Ooty to Mettupalayam, travelling more than seven thousand feet down the mountainside.

The scenery was spellbinding, to say the least. Jewel-like waterfalls dotted the hills on one side while the lush green valley dipped on the other. And flowers — there were simply hundreds of them in myriads of colours. If there is a paradise on earth, then this is probably it. I insisted on sitting on the left side of the compartment, next to the window, both ways, so as to not miss the scenery on either side.

The train stopped many times on the way, sometimes at stations and just like that during the others.

I got off the train along with Jason when it stopped immediately after crossing the Fernhill Station, as there was a lot of excited chatter which we could hear through our window.

Imagine! It was an elephant crossing the tracks. We got to know from a local that it had got separated from its herd and was on its way to join them. This is the first time I set eyes on an elephant, especially one at such close quarters.

My heart beat so hard in excitement and well, let me admit it, a little bit in fear as I held Jason's hand tightly, staring at the huge animal walking gracefully, its small tail swinging back and forth, swatting at a couple of flies which hovered at its hind side. It was all of fifteen minutes before the guard blew the whistle for the train to continue on its journey...

Jamie ran his eyes down the page, to read the last line...

While Jason teased me mercilessly, I could see he was glad I enjoyed the trip.

Goodnight!

Yours sincerely,
Barbara

Jamie closed the diary and sat at his desk, staring at the wall for a few minutes, his mind running around in circles. He had skipped the lines in between because he almost knew them by heart. His grandmother's description of the land was so vivid, especially to someone who had heard her talking about it repeatedly.

He randomly opened another page…

November 17, 1944
Dear Diary,

Our house is ready and we plan to move into it tomorrow morning. Sigh! Rose Garden is the most beautiful structure, probably because of the love Jason has poured into every single brick which went into its construction.

Why such a prosaic name for our house? All I can say is, the first time we went to check the land for this property, I could see roses growing rampantly there, all having been planted by the English people who had made Ooty their holiday home. It so reminded me of the English countryside. I couldn't think of a more apt name for our home other than Rose Garden. Well, that my mother's name was Rose made it all the easier to choose the same for our new home.

I am not sure whether the others will be able to relate to it, but I see a glow surrounding our home whenever I look at it in the morning sunlight. There's a living area on the ground floor—a central hall with two wings to the left and to the right. The left wing contains the kitchen and dining area, while the right wing houses the library which gets most of the morning sunlight. I cannot imagine living anywhere else in the world.

And oh yes! Jason and I are expecting our bundle of joy soon. The doctor confirmed I am pregnant with our first child, to be born sometime in the June of next year. Life cannot get better than this, I am sure...

Jamie paused, his mind going inward. Barbara and Jason Scott had left Ooty in the February of 1947, a little more than two years from this diary entry, along with Baby Nathan, who had been about a year and a half old. They had decided to move to Australia as there had been talks of India getting its independence from being a British colony.

"Did you never think of going back to Ooty, Granny?" Jamie had been nine when he asked Barbara that question.

"No darling. My heart overflows with the memories of my time there with your grandfather. With him passing on, I somehow never felt the urge to go back there." Jason Scott had died twenty years ago. "Maybe you would like to visit Ooty sometime. I know you'll love the place."

His grandmother had died a year later, but the thought had been seeded in young Jamie's mind. While living the busy life of a student and later when he built his career, her stories were shifted to the back of his mind. But she had left him her diaries. And recently, after moving to Alice Springs, Jamie had taken to reading Barbara's diaries off and on. He fingered the one dated 1946. He had never found the diary of 1945. Barbara had been unable to locate it. "I'm not sure, child," she had laughed. "I didn't even know these were lying in the bottom of the trunk which we brought on *Michelle*, the ship which brought us from the Madras Port in India to Port Darwin in Australia."

Jamie looked at his computer screen now, frowning at the projects which were waiting for him. And then he looked at his grandmother's diaries lying on his lap. *What should I do?*

A sudden smile tugged at Jamie's rugged face. The call of Ooty was too powerful. He had but one life to live. Might as well live his dream along with his grandmother's wishes!

When he found a hotel by the name of Rose Garden International, Jamie didn't think twice before booking a cottage for his stay. Jamie promised to take just ten days off to check his grandmother's favourite place before he got back to his regular life.

4

Rhea gave Gulliver his head as the stallion galloped across the hilly meadow, crossing over carrot fields, excited to be able to move faster at a smart trot rather than his usual smooth gait. Rhea felt a smile stretching across her face, her first natural one after what seemed like months, as the cold wind blew back her long hair, which had escaped free from the silver clip which had fallen somewhere along the way.

The hour-long ride was thoroughly exhilarating. Both rider and horse returned to the stable, pleased with their exercise. Rhea got off Gulliver's back and patted him. "Thanks buddy," she whispered into his twitching ear before handing him over to the groom. She turned to walk towards her cottage. She needed a shower before going back to the hotel.

Rhea stood in the reception hall half an hour later, her eyes falling on the foreigner who was standing at the main counter. The hotel saw a number of westerners walk in throughout the year. But something about this man's profile triggered her curiosity. Rhea walked forward and nodded her head regally at Jasmine, Anand and Sylvia who manned the reception.

Jasmine continued to verify the guest's identity on her computer after acknowledging her boss's presence. Jamie Scott had done his booking online. "Would you like to be seated, sir?" asked Jasmine politely, "while we get a photocopy of your passport and your cottage key ready?"

Jamie shrugged. "I'd like a hot toddy while I wait for the formalities to be completed. Could you help me with the order?"

"Sure sir. Any special preferences?"

"I like it spicy and served with honey."

Jamie turned swiftly from the reception and almost collided against Rhea who had been a couple of feet behind him. "Shucks!" He placed his hands on her shoulders. "I'm sorry I didn't see you." He gave her a lopsided smile, his green eyes crinkling at the corners as they studied the woman in front of him boldly. He had to exercise iron control over the tremor which passed through his body when his hands came in contact with her slender shoulders. His heart was on the verge of breaking free as it galloped wildly in his chest, while his stomach flipped in somersaults. She sure looked good enough to eat. She was taller than average, the top of her head almost touching his shoulder. She was probably in her late twenties and appeared confident, though just now, her black eyes reminded him of those of a startled deer which had been caught in the headlights of a car. Jamie gave a small shake of his head, trying to clear the buzzing in his ears.

"No harm," said Rhea, shaken by the sizzle of electricity which thrummed from where he touched her shoulders. She could feel the warmth of his hands despite the fleece-lined jacket she wore.

"Jamie Scott," he said, taking his hands off her shoulders before offering his right hand to shake hers.

"Rhea Bansal." No way could she be missing his touch! How could she? She barely knew the man. Rhea looked up into his dancing jade green eyes with her own charcoal black gaze. He was a handsome specimen of manhood with his striking features, not to mention his overgrown, dark blond locks. The thick fuzz on his cheeks gave him a rakish look; a smile playing on his mobile lips, the grooves bracketing his mouth only adding to his striking looks. Being tall herself at five feet, nine inches; it was rare indeed for Rhea to feel the need to look way up at a man. Jamie Scott must be at least four inches over six feet, she concluded.

"Good to meet you Ms Bansal. Would you like to join me for a drink?"

Rhea gave him a smile. "Maybe in the evening, Mr Scott. I'm on duty as of now."

"Oh, you work here?" Jamie had presumed she was a guest like himself. She wasn't wearing any kind of uniform or a name tag for that matter. He looked at her curiously, wondering if she held a senior position at the hotel.

"I do. I hope you have a pleasant stay at Rose Garden International, Mr Scott."

"Thank you. I plan to," said Jamie, walking away from her reluctantly, seeing that she had already taken a step away from him. He sat on a sofa, not far from the stone grate with a cheerfully roaring fire which filled the room with warmth. It was strategically positioned in the middle of the circular reception. He sat facing the reception desk as he couldn't take his eyes off Rhea Bansal. He sipped the toddy as he watched her settle into the chair behind a computer. She was attractive to say the least. It looked like his holiday in Ooty promised to be more interesting than even he had expected it to be.

Rhea was curious about their new guest. His face seemed familiar, though it was obvious he was staying at her hotel for the first time. With a small frown, she wondered why as she ran through his booking details. Jamie Scott was from Alice Springs, Australia and this was his first trip to India. Since she had never been to his country, their paths had obviously not crossed in either Australia or India. She wasn't familiar with his name either.

Well, he had Hollywood actor Chris Hemsworth's colouring, but the resemblance ended there. She had definitely seen Jamie Scott somewhere, maybe his picture on the internet. She would get to the bottom of it. He planned to stay at Rose Garden International for ten days. Good! Enough time!

It didn't strike Rhea that she was showing inordinate interest in something—okay, someone— for the first time after her hotel was up and running smoothly. She refused to dwell on the sizzle she had experienced at his touch. She had probably imagined it.

5

On the second morning of his trip, Jamie took his cup of black coffee to the balcony of his cottage. His cottage, no 96, was located at the top of the hill and Jamie could see the entire hotel stretched out in front of him in a gentle slope, the green grass and white structures appearing beautiful through the mist. The sunlight was having a difficult time breaking through the fog which shrouded the area at seven in the morning. Sipping his coffee, his elbows on the railing, Jamie turned his head to the right when he heard the clippety clop of horse hooves on the tarred road criss-crossing the property.

He had spent the whole of yesterday checking out the hotel premises and found it amazingly beautiful and well-maintained. The main business of the hotel was conducted in the towered structure with provisions stored in one wing while the other wing was well-stocked with hotel linen and toiletry items. Guests could get to see the operation if they were escorted by a management employee. While Jamie had hoped Rhea Bansal would go with him, it had been Aftab who had given him the grand tour.

Two long curved low-slung buildings were built on both sides of the main building, like brackets. The building on the left housed six shops, flanked by Bon Heur—the hotel's delicatessen, and Bugatti—the 24-hour coffee shop. "All the restaurants are named after roses," said Aftab.

The one on the right held the gymnasium, a salon, a massage parlour, with steam and sauna rooms—and of course the inevitable bathrooms.

Two large, circular, single-storied buildings were built right behind the main hotel. The first one was divided into four arcs, and housed the other restaurants. "The kitchens for all four restaurants are grouped together in the centre," Aftab pointed out to the Australian guest.

Jamie nodded. "Won't the aromas get mixed up?" he wondered loudly and turned in surprise when Aftab spoke.

"Air curtains have been created between the kitchens while the smells get absorbed by powerful chimneys. They have the added advantage of keeping insects and dust at bay," said Aftab with a smile, bringing an answering smile to the guest's face.

Jamie's eyes went wide when he stepped into the next circular enclosure behind the restaurants. A heated swimming pool of Olympic proportions was installed within, the temperature set to suit the climate. Perfect!

The cottages came after this, built in concentric circles around another circular building—way larger than the first two—in separate compounds, with flourishing gardens which had not only roses, but chrysanthemums and zinnias also growing abundantly. The building in the centre housed a banquet hall which could comfortably accommodate one thousand guests. This could again be divided into four quarters and hired as separate halls for smaller parties. Jamie was truly impressed when he saw a tunnel in the basement which connected the restaurants with the banquet hall. It was a smart idea as neither the waiters nor the food needed to get cold as they traversed the distance between the two.

The land sloped up gently from the reception to the last line of cottages, in perfect symmetry with the structures, providing an aesthetic effect. The designer in Jamie could totally appreciate the way the hotel property was built.

"Thank you Aftab," he said, shaking the management trainee's hand. "That was an amazing tour and I enjoyed every bit of it."

"You are welcome, sir," said Aftab, taking leave of the guest, refusing the tip which he was offered. The hotel levied service charges from the guests and the money collected was distributed proportionately among all the staff. They took pride in not accepting tips.

Just now, Jamie saw a horse and rider coming up the slope in the direction of his cottage which was in the last row. He felt his heartbeat pick up when he noticed Rhea on a black horse with a white star on its forehead. When he raised his hand in a wave, she slowed down to a walk and guided her horse towards him. "Good morning," Rhea called out to the Australian guest.

"Good morning, beautiful," Jamie responded in his gruff baritone, a wide smile on his handsome face. Just then, the sun's rays broke through the mist to shine on his features, surrounding him with a brilliant glow.

The breath caught in Rhea's throat as she stared at him in fascination, sliding off her horse and stepping towards the cottage railing. "I hope you're enjoying your stay with us, Mr Scott."

"Absolutely, and the name's Jamie," he replied. "Would you care to have some coffee?"

Rhea smiled. "I wouldn't say 'no'." She tied Gulliver's reins loosely to the trunk of a tree close by before climbing the three marble steps.

"Have a seat," he offered, indicating the comfortable sofas on the balcony, before turning towards the sitting room. "How do you like your coffee?"

Rhea laughed softly. "I prefer filtered coffee. Let me call room service. Would you also like some? South Indian coffee is strong and delicious. You must try it while you're here," she recommended.

Jamie shrugged. "Why not?" He went and sat next to her as she took out a walkie-talkie to place the order for a pot of filter coffee. Once she was done, he asked, "What do you do here, Rhea?"

"I manage the hotel."

Jamie was impressed. "You do? Then I must congratulate you. I've never seen a more efficiently run hotel."

Rhea's face turned red at his open praise. "Thanks, I have a great team."

"I'm sure," said Jamie, shaking his head. She was being modest. She was obviously the strong force guiding them.

"This is your first trip to India. Usually, people go to see the Taj Mahal in Agra and the palaces of Rajasthan. How come you chose to come down south to Ooty?" Rhea didn't pretend not to know the details on his passport.

"To cut a long story short, my grandmother was from England; Liverpool to be exact. She had lived in Ooty for a few years when it used to be a British colony. I've heard her talk a lot about this place. I'm on a break and decided to check out this place which my granny loved till the day she died."

Rhea looked at him in surprise. "Talk of it being a small world. It's true that Ooty was developed during the British Raj. But you're from Australia, right?" She looked at him avidly, not bothering to hide the curiosity she felt.

Jamie nodded. "My grandparents moved to Alice Springs when my dad was a toddler. This was just before India gained her independence or that's what my grandmother says in her diary."

"That was in August 1947."

"Yeah, that's right. They left Ooty in February 1947."

Just then, a golf cart came into view, bearing the order Rhea had placed. A smiling waiter wished them both a pleasant morning before he placed the silver tray with the coffee service on a low-slung table and offered the bill to Rhea.

"That would be mine," said Jamie, trying to take the bill.

Rhea shook her head, laughing softly. "Let go, Jamie." She signed the bill and sent the waiter on his way before saying, "I as good as invited myself for coffee. It's not fair asking you to pay the bill."

He nodded, watching as she poured the black coffee into the two cups placed on saucers. "I'll accept provided you have dinner with me tonight."

Rhea paused in the act of pouring milk into the cups and looked up at him with her coal black gaze. Jamie was extremely attractive and she could feel her pulse beat going high whenever she came within a few feet of him. Then again, he was a guest at her hotel. Rhea did tend to socialise with her guests pretty often, especially westerners since there was no awkwardness because she was a single woman. It went a long way in making them comfortable. The same couldn't be said of the Indian guests though. She shrugged now, with a small smile on her face. "Okay, I'll do that." Turning back to the coffee, she asked, "Do you take sugar? I would recommend milk in the coffee definitely, to have it exactly like the locals do."

Jamie nodded, pleased that she had agreed to have dinner with him, without making a fuss. "Let's have it exactly the right way, then. And I'll have one sugar."

Her fingers brushed against his, when she handed his cup and saucer to him, making her hand tremble in response. She would probably have dropped the utensils if he hadn't taken a firm hold on them.

Jamie looked deeply into Rhea's eyes as he took a sip of the coffee. He raised the cup in a toast and said, "This is brilliant. Thanks for introducing me to it."

Silence reigned for the next few minutes as they drank one more cup of coffee each, relishing every drop of it. "You must tell me what's the best food to eat here as I'm not too familiar with Indian cuisine."

"I'll recommend the Taj Mahal restaurant for Mughlai food. It has a wide range of chicken and mutton dishes richly flavoured with Indian spices and served with leavened bread or rice." Jamie nodded as she continued, "And the Gold Strike restaurant is where you get to eat Chettinadu cuisine, the dishes originating from a town by the same name. Both vegetarian and non-vegetarian dishes are equally delicious. Though it's best you tell your waiter in advance if you don't care for spicy food," warned Rhea, smiling at him.

"Thanks for the warning. Medium spice is my limit," he smiled. "And is it possible to hire a horse?"

Rhea nodded. "Of course, you can. We have half a dozen horses in our stables. Have you ever ridden before or do you plan to learn from scratch?"

Jamie grinned. "I grew up on a farm. So..." he shrugged.

Rhea smiled. "The stables are at the side, behind the shops. You'll probably have to walk a bit, or..."

"Perfect. I'll find the place. And Rhea, thanks for the coffee."

Rhea nodded, getting up from her chair, after placing the used coffee cup on the tray. "Someone will be around to pick this up. I'll be seeing you around."

"Don't forget our dinner date," called out Jamie as he watched her swing up on the horse, checking out her curvaceous butt and long legs admiringly. Getting to know her was on the top of his list now.

hea went back home to shower and change after her morning ride. After so many months, she found herself smiling from the moment she woke up. She grinned at herself in the bedroom mirror as she tucked the tails of her pin-striped shirt of black on white into her black trousers. She liked to be in control—of her life as well as of what happened around her, especially her business. All that energy had been poured into making Rose Garden International a smooth-running operation, so much so that there was no challenge in it any more. And that's exactly what had been missing in her life.

Meeting Jamie Scott had brought Rhea alive, it seemed. He was handsome and intelligent. More than that, the look in his sexy green gaze called out to her. Oh, and then there was the sizzle in his touch.

Rhea had been seventeen when she thought she was in love for the first time. Nayan had been Rohit's college mate and had visited them during the summer holidays. She had been attracted to the lanky young man from the moment she set eyes on him. Rhea had been excited when she got to go around

Mahabaleshwar with her brother and his friend. Her love for Nayan had lasted the whole of the week until the day when he tried to kiss her.

It was late evening when Nayan caught Rhea alone behind one of the guest cottages. "Hey," he called out to her.

She turned to look at him, her eyes shining and her heart in her throat. She'd never had the chance to be alone with him. "Hi," she responded, her voice breathless.

He pulled her roughly into his arms, without so much as a by-your-leave. A startled Rhea placed her hands on his chest, trying to maintain a distance. While the thought of stolen kisses had seemed exciting in her imagination, she wasn't keen on being man-handled and that was exactly what Nayan was doing.

"Let me go." Her voice was firm.

"Come on, baby. Don't play hard to get. I've been watching the way you've been eyeing me, like a cat which eyes a pot of cream."

Eow! She grimaced. That sounded so disgusting. "Let me go, Nayan."

He laughed loudly, obviously enjoying her struggle as she pushed hard to get out of his grip around her waist. He tightened his hold on her as he pulled her roughly to his chest. Rhea yelled as her breasts hurt when they were crushed against his body. Even more than her person, it was her ego which was bruised. How dare he?!

Temper exploded within her when his hand moved to the front to grope her breast, even as he pressed his wet lips on hers. She bit him, hard, drawing blood, even as she aimed a knee to his groin. Growing up with two brothers, Rhea was used to playing rough.

Nayan howled, screaming, "You bitch!" as he doubled up in pain.

Rhea laughed out loud, her face maniacal in the light of the electric lamp shining from the balcony of a cottage. She was shaking with temper and also the downward spiral of adrenaline as she did an about turn and raced towards home. She could hear him following after a minute, his steps unsteady. But she wasn't too scared. Her father and brothers would beat the bastard into pulp when they got to know what he had done to her, or at least tried to.

How had she ever imagined she was in love with this fool?!

Nayan ran away that night, fearing for his life when he faced the angry *Sardar* Alok Bansal and his strapping sons Rohit and Ritvik.

Rohit hugged his sister, stroking her hair. "I'm so sorry I brought that scum home."

She looked up at him, giving him a grin. "Didn't I do good defending myself?"

Rohit laughed. "That you did! You sure deserve a prize for that."

The second time Rhea had put her heart on the line was during her first job. Rhea had been twenty-four when she joined The Palazzo, a hotel in Bangalore, to gain experience in the hospitality industry. Sujit had been her immediate boss. They had got along well from the first day. Soon, she began to believe he was the love of her life. Sujit was decent, gentle, and treated her with respect. He was good-looking in a quiet sort of way, very different from the men in her family. But Rhea had been sure he was the man for her.

It was the time for appraisal a year later, and Rhea was confident she had done exceedingly well. An opening had come up at the hotel for the post of duty officer and she simply knew the job was hers. She decided she would take Sujit out for dinner after she received her appointment letter.

Excited, Rhea walked into The Palazzo, confident that the promotion was hers. Well, Eashwar was also in the running, but he was nowhere near as good as she was. And then, the final decision was in Sujit's hands.

The first sight which met Rhea's eyes when she went inside was Sujit shaking Eashwar's hand, before patting him on his shoulder. "Congratulations, man!"

Had she heard that right? She looked at Eashwar's jubilant face and then at Sujit. What had she missed?

Sujit turned to her and said, "Good morning, Rhea." Though he smiled at her, his eyes flitted around, refusing to settle on hers.

"Good morning, Sujit," she replied, her voice soft.

"Come over to my cabin. I need to talk to you."

Rhea followed Sujit as he went into his office, showing her a chair before shutting the door firmly.

She was quiet, trying to understand what had happened outside just now. Well, it was up to Sujit to enlighten her.

"Rhea, I've been thinking..."

"Oh yes, of course." Rhea couldn't help the sarcasm which slipped into her voice.

He gave her a startled glance. Sujit had always believed she was amiable. Had he been wrong? "You know what? I like you, a lot. So, I was thinking maybe we should get married. What do you say?"

Rhea stared at him, her jaw dropping. Was it any way to propose marriage? Huh?! Well, if he had uttered the same words yesterday, then maybe—just maybe—she might have jumped at the chance. But today morning was different.

"Are you proposing to me?" she asked, a shapely eyebrow up in query, while her expression gave away nothing.

"Of course, I am, Rhea. I want you to be my life partner," he declared in a passionate voice.

She would have laughed out loud if he hadn't sounded so pathetic! Why wasn't he holding her close to his heart if that was what he wanted? The moron was sitting in his office chair, while she was on the opposite side, the whole width of the office desk separating them.

"Can we talk about this outside our work place? I'd rather discuss my confirmation. I'm sure you understand that." Rhea's voice was firm.

"I was just getting to that. I..."

Did Sujit just squirm in his seat? Or had she been imagining it? Rhea pinned her black-as-coal gaze on his face, her own unsmiling. "Tell me."

Sujit fingered his tie as if it was strangling him, suddenly feeling hot. Where was the smiling, easy going, ever polite employee he had hired? This woman in front of him was a firebrand. What he didn't understand was that Rhea had been doing her job perfectly well as she was in guest relations. The avatar he had seen of hers had been the facet she showed the guests. He never got to know the real woman, because he had never bothered to, supremely confident that he had her exactly where he wanted her—under his thumb.

"Let's get married and..."

"Sujit, I think that's not for discussion at our place of work. I thought we just agreed on that. You were going to tell me about..."

He looked angry now. "I would, if you will stop interrupting me every time." Sujit glared at her, obviously annoyed. When she simply stared at him without saying anything, he drew in a deep breath and spoke in a persuasive voice, "Rhea, let's not argue. You know I love you. And I know you have feelings for me too. Which is the reason why I thought we should get married." He paused to see if she had anything to say.

Rhea kept the scowl off her face with difficulty, gritting her teeth, waiting for him to get to the point.

"As my wife, there's no need for you to work. You will be the queen of my heart as well as my home." He gave her a weak grin, searching for a positive response on her face.

Rhea's expression turned stony. "Oh...kay! And?"

He gave a soft laugh, a relieved expression on his face. He rubbed his hands together in pleasure, confident he had done the right thing. "Which is why I decided that Eashwar should get the job of duty officer. I know you are way better than he is. But you don't need the job anymore; while he does, and desperately too. His wedding is to take place in about two months. He needs the confirmation and the increment in salary. I'm so glad you understand."

"But what about the career I worked for?" Rhea asked, her voice dry, holding her temper back in check with great effort.

"Eh?! What career?" Sujit laughed. "Come on, Rhea. We all know you don't really need a job, not yesterday nor today. And tomorrow, when you are my wife, you most definitely get to live the life of the idle rich. You..."

"May I ask you something, Sujit?" Rhea asked, looking down at her hand, studying her long nails painted a pastel pink. "Do you really understand the difference between a job and a career?"

"Come on Rhea, what a stupid question is that! Of course, I know." Sujit laughed again, but it sounded hollow to his own ears.

She lifted her eyes suddenly to give him a glance which appeared to slice him like a laser beam. "So, what would you say about the work I was doing here? Was I doing a job or was I building a career?"

Sujit gave her a shocked look. Was she challenging him? Rhea didn't need the job or a career for that matter. What the hell was bothering her?

"Does it really matter?"

That did it! How the hell did she even imagine this moron was the man for her?

"If you had always planned to give the job to Eashwar, why did you give me the impression that I had a chance at it?" she asked mildly.

"Er... I... I thought that, that your performance..."

"You just pitched me against him, to make use of my skills. Am I right?" Rhea's tone was feral, the expression in her eyes deadly.

Sujit was sweating profusely by now. He was sure women used jobs as stop gaps before getting married. Come on, why would a woman want to go to work when she could stay at home, leading a luxurious life with her husband bringing home a good income? He seemed to have missed the human race's transition into the twenty-first century while there had been career women through the ages. He really couldn't see the need for Rhea to be angry.

"Come on, Rhea. You are good at rising to challenges. And Eashwar could do with the competition you brought to the position. He has improved a lot since you came on board, you know? I..."

"Just shut up." Rhea got up from her chair, her stance menacing, though her voice had gone quieter. "Do you even hear yourself? How dare you? How dare you make use of me like this? Do you think you can get away with it all because I am a woman? What if I tell you that I have recorded our conversation on my phone? Will you change your tune then?"

Sujit went white as he took out a handkerchief to mop his face. He had to save the situation. The woman standing in front of him looked like an avenging

Goddess. "Sit down Rhea. Can't we talk this over like two civilised people?"

"You," she pointed a finger at him, flames leaping out of her black eyes, "are not civilised. You should have talked this over with me *before* giving Eashwar the promotion, not after the event."

Sujit lost it. "You can't dictate to me on how I run this operation. I will decide who gets the job, not you." There! That should tell her who was the boss.

Rhea gave him an evil smile. "Oh really?! Are you the sole decision-maker in this huge organisation? What is the HR department for? Are they your puppets?"

"Get out of my office. You don't have a job here anymore."

"I wouldn't work in this place even if you gave me the post of the managing director, you freak," snarled Rhea, doing an about turn as she stepped out of his office.

She stopped outside the door and took a few deep breaths. She wasn't going to take this lying down. While she didn't want to work here anymore, she wasn't going to let Sujit get away with what he had done.

Rhea walked to the reception to meet Eashwar. He might be a mediocre employee, but he had landed the job, believing that he was being appreciated for his skills. She congratulated him, a smile on her face which didn't quite reach her eyes.

"Thank you, Rhea. With you around, I never thought I had a chance of landing the job. But then,

Sujit sir told me the two of you are getting married. Congrats!" Eashwar gave her a wide grin.

"Sujit presumed too much," said Rhea, not explaining herself. "I'm taking the day off. I'm sure you'll manage the desk very well now that you are the duty officer." She turned and left a shocked Eashwar spluttering incoherently.

How the hell was he going to manage the desk without her efficient assistance?

Rhea went to the top floor and waited to meet the chairman. It took half a day, but when his secretary realised that the woman was going nowhere, she managed to find a five-minute window between his many appointments.

Rhea walked into Ganesh Dasegouda's office. He recognised her immediately as the efficient woman who had been working as a trainee at his hotel for the past one year. He listened attentively when Rhea told him concisely about her grievances. "I don't want to place an official complaint sir, raking up muck. But I felt that I should report this to you. You will be able to find a record of my achievements with the HR. In a way I am glad I didn't get the job. I would never work in a place where women aren't respected."

Dasegouda listened to her, nodding wisely. "I'd be extremely sorry to see you go, Rhea Bansal. You are an asset to any hotel. Do think about it. I can definitely give you a better placement. What do you say?"

"Thank you, sir. That's really nice of you. But no, it's time to move on. My brother has set up a hotel in

Mumbai. I will go to work with him. He's been asking me to join him since a long time. But I thought I would get to do plenty of work and learn more outside a family environment."

"Is it? Which hotel is this?"

"Simha International. It's new. I..."

"Are you Rohit Bansal's sister?" The chairman looked astounded.

"Do you know him?" Rhea smiled. She was absolutely proud of her brother even otherwise, but the recognition in her boss's eyes for him multiplied the feeling manifold.

"Not personally, no. But everyone in the hotel circles has heard of him for sure. And thank you for bringing this matter to my notice, Rhea. I wish you the very best in your future endeavours. I'm confident you'll do very well."

Rhea got up. "Thank you, sir. And goodbye!"

Sujit couldn't believe his ears when he got a call from the chairman's secretary. Worse was yet to come. Ganesh Dasegouda didn't bother to dismiss him. Sujit felt that that would have been better when he found out he had been demoted to the position of night manager, with Eashwar as his assistant.

"Rhea Bansal is lying, sir. You shouldn't believe a word she says," he grumbled when he came face to face with his boss.

A salt and pepper eyebrow went up on hearing this. "You think so? But she was all praise for you. Does it mean you don't deserve any of that?" The old man was too crafty for Sujit who gave him a confused look.

"What did she say?" asked Sujit curiously.

"Whatever! I take it I shouldn't believe her. Isn't that what you said just now?"

"Sir, please. Why are you making me a night manager? Haven't I been doing my job well?" Sujit whined in desperation.

"Of course, you have, Sujit. Which is why I thought it's best you handle the night traffic into the hotel as that definitely needs an expert."

Sujit stared at the other man, opening and closing his mouth rapidly, no words coming out of his mouth. "I... I don't understand."

"Go Sujit. You will know by and by."

"I'm sure Rhea Bansal has poisoned your mind against me, sir." Sujit had known through some of the staff in the chairman's office that she had met the old man. "I'll get her for this."

Ganesh Dasegouda laughed softly. "Are you suggesting I am foolish enough to fall for a pack of lies?" he asked, mild sarcasm in his voice. "And by the way, have you heard of Rohit Bansal from Mumbai?"

Sujit's eyes popped out as he replied reverently, "Of course I have heard of the hotel mogul, sir. Simha International's MD, right? What of him?"

The chairman shrugged. "Nothing much. Just that he happens to be Rhea Bansal's brother."

Sujit groaned, dropping his head in his hands, totally shaken.

"Cheer up, my boy. Be happy that you still have a job at The Palazzo," said Dasegouda, getting up from his chair to walk out of his office.

That night, due to an emergency at the hotel—a mix up in the cottages allotted to twenty guests—Rhea couldn't keep her dinner date with Jamie, much to both their disappointment.

After being introduced to South Indian filter coffee by Rhea, Jamie got ready swiftly before going out. He stopped for a continental breakfast at Bugatti before hiring a hotel car to drop him at the main market area in Ooty. He strolled around the area for half an hour, checking out the shops before going to the railway station where he planned to take a ride on the toy train. It was a glorious morning with a biting chill to the air. It took him less than ten minutes to reach the station from the market.

Nilgiri Mountain Railway! He knew that Nilgiri meant blue mountains and when he sat on the left side of the wooden seat—the same side on which his grandmother had sat, more than seventy years ago—he could well understand why the mountains were called that. A blue hue pervaded the atmosphere as the little train chugged its way gently down the mountain side.

He had found out that the morning train was going only as far as Coonoor, about an hour and twenty minutes from Ooty. Which was about half the length of the entire journey his grandparents had taken so many decades back.

He stared at the green fields of tea and coffee clinging to the mountain side and the eucalyptus trees which grew on the hills by the droves. An ice-cold breeze blew through the window. The train wasn't all that crowded. All those who were on board were tucked into their warmest clothes, right from the top of their heads to the tips of their toes. Jamie loved cold weather and kept the window on his side open, despite having his nose almost frozen and turning a bright shade of red. He grinned, thinking of the ride his grandparents must have taken on the same route. The area was more developed and definitely the trees must be way older, but the terrain was the same. And the thought gave him such immense joy.

Monkeys turned up from time to time, chasing the train as they swung along trees and bushes not far from the track. While cattle and sheep grazed in some areas, Jamie got to see many horses too. But he met no elephant to his disappointment nor was there any untoward incident to hold up the train. He had a cup of hot tea along with his co-passengers when the train stopped at the Wellington station. Though it was a bit too sweet for his taste, he relished the hot beverage.

Coonoor was the final stop. Jamie got off the train along with the others and walked over to the ticket window to find out the train timing to Mettupalayam, the final destination of the Nilgiri Mountain Railway. "There is a train at 4.15 in the evening."

Jamie nodded. "And when is the last train back to Ooty from there?"

"There's only one train from Mettupalayam to Ooty, mister. That's at 7.10 in the mornings."

Jamie nodded again, thinking. He wanted to get back to Ooty in time for his dinner date with Rhea. He came to a quick decision and bought a train ticket to Mettupalayam in the evening and left the station. He would take a cab back to Ooty.

He decided to check out the main attractions of Coonoor. Doing a search on Google Maps, he headed to SIM's Park, riding an auto-rickshaw from the station to his destination. This area of abundant greenery had found a mention in Barbara's diary, which is why it interested Jamie.

He paid the rickshaw driver, purchased a ticket and went inside the park which sloped down from the entrance. He walked around, taking in the breath-taking vista, checking out the age-old trees—some of them more than a hundred years old, according to the name boards nailed to them—and flowering shrubs. There was also a greenhouse which was home to a large variety of rose bushes and other plants. Even more than the greenery, Jamie enjoyed the rigorous walk in the cold weather, first going down and then climbing back up the slope. The highlight of the outing was the scenery which met his eyes at the end of the park. Standing there, Jamie had a three-hundred-and-sixty-degree view of the entire area from a height of over six thousand feet.

It was past 1.30 when Jamie reached Ramakrishna Lunch Home. Someone he had met in the park had mentioned that the restaurant served authentic local cuisine.

Walking in, Jamie headed to the first floor, even as people around him stared. It wasn't often when a Westerner stopped at this eatery. But the manager spoke excellent English. "We serve food on a banana leaf," he explained after Jamie settled down, once he had washed his hands thoroughly. "It's pure vegetarian."

Jamie nodded his golden head. "I've heard about that, mate. I hope you have a spoon to spare though, just in case." A grin broke out on his handsome face.

"Of course, yes." The manager directed a server to place a large leaf on the table in front of the guest. "Where do you come from?"

"Australia, Alice Springs to be exact."

"You are on holiday?"

"Yeah." Two men brought different cooked vegetables and curries and served them on the leaf as Jamie watched in fascination. He spooned the dishes one by one into his mouth and tasted them, liking the strange flavours. "Hmm... nice."

The manager grinned, happy with the exalted guest's response. "More than five hundred people have lunch here, every day, and we have around the same number for dinner."

Jamie looked around, rather amazed. The place wasn't all that big and could seat around fifty people at one go. He raised a hand to stop the server from pouring hot curry over the rice which had been served in the centre of his leaf. "May I have that in a cup, please?"

The server looked up at the manager, unable to comprehend. "*Naalu kinnam kondu vaa*," the manager told him, and the man rushed back with four stainless steel cups. They served four different types of curries in those. "That's *sambar*," explained the manager to an attentive Jamie, pointing to the first cup. "You mix it with the rice and eat, along with this fried disc," he pointed to the fried *pappadam* which had also been served on the leaf by now. "You can also have the *rasam* and *moru* with the rice, though separately each time." Jamie noted that those items were in cup two and three.

"I like *sambar*," said Jamie, working his tongue around the word, bringing a smile to the other man's face. "May I have some more?"

"Sure. Subbu, bring some more *sambar* for sir," he called out in Tamil, before continuing, "The last cup here contains *payasam*, a sweet dish. You can have that in the end."

"That's for dessert I suppose," said Jamie, before sipping from the cup of *rasam*. He thought it was too watery to mix well with the rice. Liking the taste, he drank the whole cup and asked for a second helping of that too.

Seeing how much the guest relished the food, the manager asked, "How long are you staying in Ooty? You must come again."

"I'd love to," said Jamie, smiling as he finished his dessert. "That was a truly delicious meal, mate. It could even persuade one to become a vegetarian," he said, a twinkle in his eyes.

The manager laughed. "Why not!"

Finishing the meal, Jamie got up to shake hands with the older man before going down the stairs. It was time to go to the railway station to catch the train further down to Mettupalayam. On the way, he called Rose Garden International to speak to Jasmine. "Hi, this is Jamie Scott."

"Hello sir, how may I help you?"

"I need a car from Mettupalayam back to the hotel. Will it be possible for you to arrange one for me?"

"Of course, Mr Scott. What time would that be?"

"Five-ish?"

"Let me call you again in five minutes," said Jasmine.

Jamie walked the short distance to the station and hung around there, studying the few locals who were also waiting for the same train.

Jasmine called him to confirm the car booking. "You'll get a message with the taxi registration number, the name of the driver and his cell number even as we talk, sir," said Jasmine.

"Thanks, Jasmine. How long do you think it should take to get back by road?"

"A little more than two hours."

"Perfect! Bye," said Jamie, disconnecting the phone even as the Nilgiri Mountain train chugged into the station. He got in to sit on the wooden seat, close to the window, enjoying more of the panoramic views on the way. A great day spent sightseeing, but he couldn't wait to get back to keep his dinner date with Rhea.

The ride back to Ooty was without incident as Jamie made a few calls and also completed some pending work. It was barely half an hour before he reached Rose Garden International when his phone pinged. There was a WhatsApp message from a strange number. "Hi, this is Rhea. I'm sorry I won't be able to make dinner tonight due to work. I can't get off before ten."

"Shit!" Jamie swore under his breath, startling the driver.

"You said something, sir?" said the man, looking at his passenger in the rear-view mirror.

Jamie shook his head impatiently. "Nothing." He had so wanted to spend some time with the woman and get to know her. From what he had seen and heard; Rhea worked way too hard. But would she listen to Jamie if he asked her to leave her precious work and go out with him for a couple of hours? Somehow, he didn't think so.

A new thought was born! Maybe he should extend his stay in Ooty, not his holiday, but his stay. He had his laptop with him to keep in touch with prospective clients. What if he looked for projects in the area? That would surely give him time to get to know Rhea. It was time to rent a house in Ooty. It wasn't practical to live in the 5-star hotel in the long run. With that decision made, Jamie calmed down even as they reached the ornate gates which opened to let his cab inside. He guided the driver to his cottage, signed the bill and waved him off before going inside.

Jamie went for a swim in the heated pool, doing a few laps before floating lazily on his back. He had had too much exercise that day, but it wasn't all that late and he was too wound up to go to bed. He had never felt lonely in his life. But it looked like he could miss someone, badly.

He climbed out of the pool and went to shower and change. He'd go to the hotel reception and tackle Rhea. If she was too busy, he intended to hang out there, watching her.

Jamie had got it bad, for sure!

Rhea didn't realise she had been looking out for him. But her heart picked up tempo when Jamie entered the reception from a side door. Dressed in a pair of dark blue jeans and a jade green full-sleeved t-shirt, the same shade as his eyes, he was truly a sight for sore eyes. She had put in too many hours at work and had been sorry to cancel their dinner plans. It was almost 9 pm and she needed to eat. She wondered if he had had his dinner. Well, the only way to find out was to ask.

She walked forward to meet him halfway, giving him a soft smile. "Hey!" His hair was damp, probably from a shower, she thought. His eyes were red-rimmed. Would he be too tired to spend an hour or so with her?

Jamie looked at Rhea. Though beautiful, she looked beat. "Hey," he grinned, "Are you still working?"

She shook her head. "Just got done. Have you had your dinner?"

"Nope. And you?"

Rhea grinned now. "Not yet. I know it's rather late. But would you mind sharing a meal with me?"

Jamie laughed. "I ne'er stopped hoping. Do you want to go out? Any specific place in mind?"

Rhea shook her head. "The local joints will be closing as we talk. Actually, if you don't mind, shall we order a meal over at my place? We'll order whatever you want to have," she tempted him.

Would he mind?! Jamie jumped at the chance. "I'm game. Lead me."

Rhea laughed, thrilled at his response. "Come along then." She took his hand to walk to the other end of the reception and stepped out into the cold air. "Are you okay? It's so cold."

Jamie shrugged, holding on to her hand, liking the feel of it. "I just had a swim in the hot pool. I must say it was a fabulous experience."

No wonder his hair was still damp. "I'm glad you're enjoying the hotel's facilities. So, where did you go for the day?"

They had reached the wicket gate by now. Jamie opened the latch and let her walk ahead of him, following right behind her. "I took the toy train and went all the way down the mountains."

Rhea opened the double door with a brass key. "Welcome to my home," she said, walking in.

Jamie stared, his jaw dropping. From the outside, the building had appeared like a small cottage with a tiled roof. But they had entered a living room which seemed to go on forever. "This is lovely," he said, turning to look at her.

"Make yourself at home, Jamie," she said, pointing him to a comfortable couch. "What would you like to drink?"

"Some brandy, if you have it."

"Brandy it is. Soda?" asked Rhea, turning to a well-stocked bar to remove a glass from a shelf.

Jamie walked up to her, wondering how many people lived in the house. The bar seemed to have a large collection of liquor. Seeing his gaze on them, Rhea laughed. "I have two brothers who love their drinks, just like our father. It was Ritvik who insisted on adding all that stuff."

"Do they live here?"

Rhea turned around from the fridge from where she had been getting some ice cubes. "No. It's only me."

She managed the hotel, she had said. Jamie brushed away his curiosity about the size of her abode. He took the bottle of soda from her hand and opened it before pouring it over the brandy and ice in his glass. "Aren't you having anything?"

"I plan to. But I desperately need a shower before that. Let me light the fire before going to have one. Just give me ten minutes." While there was central heating, Rhea had always thought a fire was way more fun.

"Why don't you go and have your shower? I'll light the fire," offered Jamie.

"Are you sure?"

Jamie grinned. "Of course! And I'll keep your drink ready for you. What's your poison?"

"Hmm... I'm wondering. I prefer cocktails. Maybe I'll order something from the hotel."

"Allow me. I'll make a cocktail for you. Something sweet or you prefer tangy?"

"A bit of both? With lots of ice. That'd be awesome. I'll see you soon," she said, walking to the left side and disappearing through a doorway.

Jamie took a sip of his brandy before going to the grate. Logs were neatly piled and ready to be lit. He took some kindling and set it going in no time. No, he wasn't going to think of a nude Rhea standing under the shower. Shaking his head, Jamie went to the bar and removed a tall glass and filled half of it with crushed ice. Adding some vodka, raspberry liqueur and amaretto liqueur, he squeezed the juice of half a lemon into it. He topped it with lemon-lime soda and stirred the drink, all set for Rhea.

Taking his own glass, Jamie walked to the floor-length window overlooking the hotel which seemed like something out of a fairy tale. He gazed at it unseeingly, sipping from his glass. He couldn't wait for Rhea to join him.

He turned around when he felt her presence and stared unblinking at the sveltely-clad woman who had walked back into the living room in exactly ten minutes as promised. The length of her graceful legs was enhanced by white stilettos. Her chiffon dress of deep red with a swirling white pattern fell a few inches short of her knees. Her curly hair tumbled down her shoulders all the way to her waist. Jamie lifted her cocktail glass and walked over to her, his eyes never leaving her face.

Rhea's breath was coming in soft gasps. She had made an effort to dress up after a long, long time; it had been a while since she had felt the urge to. A sizzle went up her arm when her fingers brushed against his as she took the drink from him. "Cheers!" Her voice hoarse, she raised the glass in a toast, touching it to his.

"Cheers!" he echoed her, sitting down after she took a seat.

Rhea took a sip from her glass, her eyes shut in concentration, more because of the sudden bout of shyness which had attacked her when she noticed the fire in his green gaze. "Mmm... this is delicious." She opened her slumberous black gaze to look at him, "Though lethal," she smiled. "What's in it?"

He shook his golden head. "I'm not telling. Do you like it? Or would you rather have something else?"

"I love it. Though one is more than enough at a time, I think."

He grinned. "You're right. It's kinda strong."

Rhea took a couple of more sips before keeping her glass down. "What would you like to have for dinner? I had a menu card here somewhere. Let me go get it."

Jamie raised a hand to stop her. "Don't bother to get up. Tell me what you recommend. I like all kinds of food generally. I'll go with your choice."

"Okay, I'll place the order then." She got up to get her walkie-talkie and spoke into it. "Half an hour and we'll have a grand meal."

"That's pretty fast service. Do you people have home delivery too?" asked Jamie, his expression curious. It was a 5-star and he guessed not.

Rhea smiled. "No, our services don't stretch that far."

"You must be special then."

"I suppose I am."

"Who are you, Rhea Bansal?"

She looked at him shrewdly. She never said it, unless pushed into a corner. But well... with a mental shrug, she replied, "I own more than half of Rose Garden International and work there in the capacity of managing director." She hadn't made the mistake Rohit had done and she was lucky she had a rich brother to invest in her hotel when it was a start-up. Being the control freak that she was, Rhea had ensured that seventy-five per cent of the shares remained within the family in which her personal stake was fifty-one per cent.

"Aah!" Jamie's eyes lit up. "And a hardworking MD at that, I see."

Rhea tilted her head in acknowledgement. "I suppose. I enjoy every second of it, so I can't say it's all *hard* work. More like *joy* work."

Jamie was impressed by her attitude, watching her avidly as he drank from his glass.

"And what do you do, Jamie?" she asked.

"I design interiors. I have done hotels and corporate houses so far."

"How lovely! So, what do you think of our hotel?"

"It's perfect," he declared, making her go red in the face. "What? Who designed it?"

"I did." She spoke so softly that he had to bend his head close to her to catch the words.

His eyes went wide before he grinned. "I hope you aren't going to put me out of business."

She shook her head at him, smiling in response. "You don't mean that! This is just one project and that too only because it's my baby. I'm sure you're way beyond my league. Will it be possible to see your work online?"

Jamie nodded as he could see it wasn't just idle curiosity but genuine interest on her part. "Sure. I will send you a couple of links if you give me your email ID. Better yet, why don't you come over to my cottage tomorrow? I'll show you myself." It was a damn good excuse to meet her again.

"I'll do that. Unless you're going sightseeing again tomorrow."

"Maybe later in the day," Jamie shrugged. "Coffee in the morning?"

"Perfect. Do you want to go riding before that?"

This is getting better and better, thought Jamie as he nodded. "What time?"

"Meet me at the stables at 5.30 am?"

"I will."

Their dinner came and Jamie tucked heartily into the chicken curry and rice. "I suppose all Indians are rice-eaters," he said, relishing the meal.

Rhea shook her head. "Not all. Rice is the staple in the south. The North Indians have *roti*, leavened bread made from wheat flour."

Jamie nodded. "Okay."

"Have you had the chance to taste *roti*?" When he shook his head, she offered to order one for him.

"No please. I'm good. Don't want to eat any more. I'm looking forward to the dessert though. Is it *payasam*?" he asked, tongue-in-cheek.

Rhea laughed. "Where did you have that?"

"Ramakrishna Lunch Home at Coonoor, today for lunch," he grinned.

"Well, you're in for disappointment. I have only *gulab jamoon* to offer," she winked.

"Aww, let me check it out first." He took the small bowl she offered and forked a piece of the soft dessert into his mouth. "Hey, this is truly yum."

"I'm glad you think so. You can have another piece from mine too. I'm not too fond of sweets."

"I don't mind at all," said Jamie, helping himself from her bowl too.

They sat back for another half an hour, chatting like old friends. "So, you're from a family of hoteliers?"

Rhea nodded. "Yep, my parents have been running Bansal Resort at Mahabaleshwar for over forty-five years. Rohit, my elder brother, runs Simha International in Mumbai. Ritvik is the youngest of us. He's in charge of Maharaja International in Udaipur. What about your family? Where do they live?"

"In Brisbane. My parents live in a house on the beach. I have three brothers, all of them older than me and married, with kids. I had three nieces and two nephews at the last count," Jamie grinned.

"You're the baby of the family," she smiled, "But you don't live in Brisbane." His passport had said otherwise.

"You're right. I prefer to live in Alice Springs since my grandparents used to live there on a farm. Staying there during holidays, I gathered some of the best memories of my life. My father shifted to Brisbane because his work took him there. The rest of the clan likes living by the sea." He shrugged.

"Don't you get lonely with your family so far away?"

Jamie shook his head. "Not really. Anyway, I get to see them at least three to four times in a year, as I'm my own boss. And what about you? Is Mahabaleshwar very far from here?"

"It'll take me a whole day to reach my parents. But well, I need my independence. I thought it's best to move far away," she grinned. "I fell in love with Ooty and especially the bungalow which is the main office of the hotel today."

"I guess." He could see Rhea was pretty independent while she was doing a damn good job of running the hotel.

"Thanks for the wonderful company, drinks and dinner, in that order, Rhea," said Jamie, getting up from the sofa when there was a lull in the conversation. "I must be going. It's been a really long day. I look forward to our morning ride."

"Same here, Jamie. I'll see you in the morning." Rhea got up to walk him to the entrance.

Jamie opened the door and turned around to say bye, only to find her standing in the doorway, shivering. "Hey, you'd better shut the door soon." But he found he didn't have the heart to part with her. Raising his left hand, he gently stroked her right cheek with a knuckle, finding her skin silky to the touch.

Rhea shut her eyes, forgetting to breathe as she felt his light touch on her face. What would it be like if he kissed her? She realised she had never been kissed, unless she counted that horrid experience with Rohit's college-mate. But the moment was lost when Jamie walked away after wishing her goodnight. Rhea shut the door and leaned back against it, a hand on her cheek, lost in the memory of his touch.

Jamie was at the stable a few minutes before their appointed hour. There were six horses in all, including Rhea's Gulliver. He had brought along some carrots with leaves which were fresh from the farm.

He stopped at the stall next to Gulliver's where a dark brown horse with white ears and hooves stood majestically, snorting at him in greeting. "Hello," called out Jamie softly, offering a carrot to the horse, wondering what his name was.

"That's Sovereign, just the horse I was going to suggest for you," said Rhea from behind. "Good morning."

Jamie turned around to give her a smile, saying, "Good morning," in reply. She looked gorgeous, dressed in all black—her jeans, hoodie and shoes. He laughed when Sovereign butted his shoulder with his muzzle, turning around to feed the horse another carrot.

"Oh, you got carrots for the horses. How lovely!" Rhea took a few from his hand and fed Gulliver who had been watching jealously from the neighbouring stall. Soon, the other horses caught the smell and began to neigh.

Laughing, both Rhea and Jamie went around feeding the lot of them. Luckily, the earlier evening, Jamie had stopped at a roadside vendor and purchased a few bunches, just for the horses.

They saddled Gulliver and Sovereign and set off after a few minutes. "Are you familiar with the area? Do you want to go anywhere in particular?" asked Rhea, looking at her dashing companion. He sat well on the horse, his touch light on the reins.

Jamie shook his head. "Nope. I haven't had a chance to get much around Ooty. What do you suggest?" He had thought to rush headlong into daily tours when he had planned his trip. But after deciding to stay back longer, he had chosen to take it one day at a time.

Rhea was already guiding her horse up the slope towards the back of the property, Jamie walking his horse right next to her. "There's a gate at the back of the hotel which leads to a narrow lane. There won't be much traffic this early in the morning. We can gallop the horses to our hearts' content in that area."

"Perfect," said Jamie, watching her avidly. Decisive and precise, that's what she was. He bent forward to open the latch of the gate and followed her through before turning around to shut it.

Chivalrous without being pushy! Rhea was impressed.

They had a great time galloping across the fields over the next hour before returning to Jamie's cottage for coffee. This time it was Jamie who placed the order for the filter blend before he went in to get his laptop. He opened his website and turned the laptop towards Rhea who was sitting on an adjacent sofa in the balcony. While it was bitingly cold, the two of them were feeling rather warm now after their exhilarating ride.

Rhea pushed back the hood of her sweatshirt before checking out Jamie's website. Silence reigned for a while as she scrolled through the different themes Jamie had drawn up for his clients. "So, how does this work? You do the ideation from scratch or do you take your clients' inputs into consideration?" Rhea took her eyes off the laptop to look up at the silent Jamie.

"It works both ways. The hotel which you see," he said, pulling his sofa closer to the table so that he could point it out to her and continued when she nodded, "They gave me carte blanche with their project and the latest corporate that I dealt with—the owner had a number of ideas which I incorporated into the design."

Rhea nodded. "I must say they look amazing, Jamie. Thanks for showing me this."

Ruddy colour ran up Jamie's hard cheeks as he looked back at Rhea. While he was used to praise in his line of work, it felt good hearing it from her. The woman was growing on him, slowly but steadily. Just now she glowed in the misty morning, her cheeks flushed from the rigorous exercise. It was an effort not to pull her into his arms and make love to her. Was he glad when a waiter brought over the coffee!

Jamie poured the coffee exactly the way he had seen Rhea do it the earlier day. Handing her a cup and saucer, he waited for her to taste it. "Did I get the mix right?"

Rhea grinned teasingly. "Not at all bad for a first attempt," she winked. It was perfect actually.

Jamie sipped on his, a frown of concentration on his handsome features. "Hey, you're pulling my leg. It's splendid." He gave her a mock glare.

Rhea burst out laughing. "I suppose I am."

Jamie stared, his coffee forgotten, his body heating up as his heart hammered against his chest. While last night had been fun, this was the first time he saw Rhea laughing wholeheartedly. She was a sight to behold. Without really being aware of what he was doing, Jamie took her hand which was lying on her lap and held it in both of his. Staring at the long fingers with unpainted nails, he traced a thumb over the back of her hand. "You look beautiful," he said in a whisper, suddenly lifting his eyes and staring deeply into her black gaze.

Rhea stared right back, forgetting to breathe, even as her bouncing heart seemed to have lodged itself somewhere in her throat. "Jamie..." She curled her fingers around his large hand, pressing her palm against his.

Jamie leaned forward, his breath stirring the tendrils of hair at her temple, to whisper in her ear. "Rhea, do you feel it too, this powerful attraction which shakes me to the core of my being?"

Rhea took a deep, shuddering breath, fighting to keep her sanity. He was weaving magic over her, with just his words. She opened heavy eyelids to look into his eyes which were so close that she could see the pupils stretching and contracting as he stared at her, his breathing uneven. She gave a small nod after what seemed like a long time to Jamie.

"I want to know you more. I'm planning to extend my trip..."

Her eyes went wide as she continued to stare at him, colour rushing into her cheeks. She had been thinking of the time he would disappear from her life in a week's time. It looked like that wasn't a hurdle any more. She smiled at him suddenly. "That would be awesome Jamie. Though I... I..." Rhea's voice shook before she paused, willing it to steady. "Well, let me be truthful. I've got a poor track record when it comes to relationships," she grimaced before continuing, "I don't really know how..."

"Shall we take it one day at a time?" asked Jamie, his expression turning gentle as he noticed the anguish on her pretty face. "Let's see where this takes us." While he couldn't help wondering what must have happened to sour her relationships with other men, that question was for another day.

Rhea nodded again, a smile lighting up her face. "I'm glad you are going to stay longer," she said softly.

A golf cart turned up from the left of his cottage just when Jamie got up to pull her into his arms. "Shit," he swore before letting go off her hand.

A waiter got off to collect their coffee tray and left almost immediately.

Rhea grinned at Jamie, her eyes dancing. "All for the best! I need to go. Are you riding back to the stable on Sovereign or do you want me to lead him there?"

Jamie looked at her mischievous face, his face breaking out in a grin in response. "It'd be great if you could do that. I need to go out, hunting for some information and a rental home. I'll be seeing you around lunch time."

She nodded at him before climbing on Gulliver, gathering Sovereign's reins also in her hand, a light-hearted smile on her face. It was but a short ride to the stables.

Rhea liked Jamie, a lot.

10

Police Inspector Kamalakannan was keen to have lunch at Gold Strike. The food there—adapted from the cuisine of his hometown Chettinadu—was even better than what his mother used to make when he was a young boy. But the prices were atrociously exorbitant. Well, he was a policeman, someone who took care of the safety of the city in which the hotel was built. Shouldn't they feed him for free?

The only time he got to have dinner there with his family, the manager had had them thrown out before they could finish the dessert. But—Kamalakannan grinned to himself—that night he had saved more than twelve thousand rupees by not paying the bill for the five of them, including himself, his wife and his three children, even though they had to forgo the dessert. He had been banned from entering the premises. He knew Rose Garden International was owned by a mere woman. He planned to return, definitely.

KK, as Kamalakannan was also known, was shameless like that, but his temper simmered every time he recalled the insult, which was often. He was well-respected in the police circles. What he didn't realise was that it was fear which his colleagues felt towards him rather than respect. He bided his time. People forgot things. They probably would not even remember his face after four months.

What Kamalakannan wasn't aware was that the computer in the security cabin at the entrance had pictures and names of people who were banned from stepping into the portal. While it mostly consisted of goons who were wanted by the police, it also had the name and photo of this particular gentleman who worked for the police department.

The one time he had got away, Kamalakannan had been in uniform. After that, he had tried to enter the premises in civilian clothes. It hadn't worked as the security personnel refused to let him in. They had been polite but firm in their refusal.

The bitch! Rhea Bansal wasn't even a local, but from Maharashtra. How dare she challenge his authority?! Kamalakannan didn't know she had been in touch with the Commissioner of Police and their office had offered full support, just in case he caused further trouble. He had tried, a few times, without success, sending policemen to check on licenses and other things. Nothing seemed to work.

Recently, Kamalakannan had befriended a local politician. MLA Marudhanayagam had become very influential in barely two years of his tenure. He planned to visit the hotel along with the MLA. *Let them try to stop me from entering then,* Kamalakannan smirked to himself, proud of his plan.

"Good afternoon, sir," said Kamalakannan, saluting the politician. They both were about the same age, in their forties. "Have you had lunch?" It was just 12.30 and Kamalakannan was confident the other man wouldn't have had his meal.

"Tell me KK," said the MLA impatiently. "What brings you here?"

Kamalakannan's face darkened in anger which he held back with difficulty. Gritting his teeth, he gave the other man a wide smile, saying, "I was wondering if you would like to go out for lunch with me, sir. My treat," he added hastily.

Marudhanayagam's frown disappeared, to be replaced by a small smile. "So where were you thinking of going?" he asked, smacking his lips.

"Gold Strike is a restaurant at Rose Garden International, a new 5-star hotel. Have you been there?"

The MLA shut his file before turning to Kamalakannan, curious to know more. "I have heard of the place, though I've never had an opportunity to go there. It's not even four years old, right?"

Kamalakannan's gaze was sly as he nodded, excited he had the politician's complete attention. "Yes sir. It's the newest in Ooty. And do you know something? The owner is a lady. The food is excellent, in all of the five restaurants. I've heard that the cake shop is the best in Ooty."

"Really? I must go there then. Let me see..." The MLA opened his file again.

"What sir! I just told you I'll take you for lunch at Gold Strike. Which is why..."

"The prices must be exorbitant, KK. I don't mean to offend, but how can you afford it?" He refused to look up from his file now, much to the policeman's disappointment.

"A policeman can afford anything, sir. That's the kind of influence we wield," said Kamalakannan, grinning at the other man, a proud look on his face. "People are eager to give us free meals, wherever we go. We..."

"Then why don't you go and enjoy yourself?" asked the MLA, an envious look on his face. Even if the government paid all his bills, the life of a policeman appeared rosy all of a sudden. Imagine getting everything for free, especially 5-star meals.

"Come on sir. I want you to experience the food they serve there. You are from Chettinadu and I am also from there. The *pepper chicken* and *fried crab* they serve there are fit to feed a king." Kamalakannan wiped the back of his hand against his mouth, effectively stopping the drool from flowing out as he recalled his only experience. "It's even better than what my mother used to make."

Marudhanayagam shut his file decisively. "Let's go then. Your treat, you said? Do they serve drinks?" he asked, getting up. What the hell! It was Friday afternoon. He would have a few drinks and a delicious meal before heading home for a long nap.

"The finest sir," said Kamalakannan, thrilled now. Let the security personnel stop the MLA and his friend, he thought to himself with a wicked grin.

Rhea kept a look out for the dark blue sedan with the number plate TN 27 MG 4545 from behind the double glass door at the reception. The security guard had made a desperate call directly to her claiming that the trouble making police inspector was back along with an MLA in tow. He hadn't known how to stop them without offending the politician.

Rhea decided that today was the last day the policeman showed his face at her hotel. She had already called the police commissioner's office for backup.

When the car stopped at the portico, Rhea walked out to greet the two men who got out of the car from either side.

"Welcome to Rose Garden International, gentlemen," greeted Rhea, her expression pleasant even as she fumed within.

"What a lovely welcome from a beautiful woman," said Marudhanayagam, a leer on his face as he ran his eyes up and down her slender figure encased in western formals.

Even though Rhea was covered from neck to feet, she felt besmirched by his lascivious gaze. Gritting her teeth, she continued as if she hadn't heard him, "If I may have a few minutes of your time in my office, please?"

While Kamalakannan's gaze turned wary as warning bells rang in his head, the MLA jumped at the chance to spend some time with her in the privacy of her office, even as he wondered how to get rid of his policeman friend. His mind working furiously, he gave her a wide grin before nodding vigorously. "Of course, madam, it would be my pleasure."

Kamalakannan wanted to warn the other man that they were probably walking into a trap, but the politician had no eyes for anyone other than the vision which walked by his side. He stared openly at her chest, disgusted at the many layers of clothing she wore. Despite all that, he could not miss her luscious figure. He had to make her his, come hell or high water.

Rhea held her hands in fists which itched to smash into his face. Yes, she was a trained fighter and could wield a punch effectively these days. But the man was an MLA damn it, and a guest at her hotel just now. She opened the door to her office and went behind her desk, inviting the two men to sit down. Lifting the phone, she requested Anand to send Vadivel inside.

While Marudhanayagam continued to drool at Rhea, Kamalakannan was on pins. "Good afternoon, gentlemen. Could you please tell me the purpose of your visit to the hotel?" asked Rhea, opening the conversation.

"Eh?!" It finally struck the MLA that everything wasn't as it should be. "I don't understand. Why would someone visit a hotel?" he asked icily even as temper flared in his eyes.

Rhea gave him a menacing smile. "You'll need to tell me that. The police officer accompanying you, are you aware he's been banned from entering the premises? And do you know why?" she asked, relieved to see the lock turning to let Officer Vadivel from the police commissioner's office in. He stood there without saying a word, watching the proceedings.

Kamalakannan could sense that someone else had come in and was desperate to find out who it was. But his ego wouldn't let him take his eyes off the woman who was challenging the MLA. This was drama at its best. Marudhanayagam would never take this lying down.

"I don't know what you are talking about. How can you ban someone? Isn't it a free country?" asked Marudhanayagam challengingly. While he wouldn't admit it to the woman in front of him, he was furious with Kamalakannan. The bastard hadn't told him he was banned from the premises.

"You are right, it's a free country and everyone's welcome to roam around. But this hotel belongs to a private company and yes, we do have the right to stop troublemakers from entering." Rhea's voice was firm.

"Is it? So, are you suggesting that Inspector Kamalakannan is a troublemaker?"

"I am not suggesting it, sir. I am *declaring* it is so. He wasn't stopped at the gate because he was in your company. Otherwise..."

Marudhanayagam's face lit up as he presumed that to be a compliment. "Oh! Is that how it is? Will you allow him to remain just this once? I'll make sure he behaves," he offered, giving her a leery smile.

"Which is exactly the reason I am keen to know the purpose of your visit."

The MLA frowned heavily. How dare she question his moves! Gritting his teeth, he said, "We are planning to have lunch here."

"And who's going to pay the bill?" she asked.

Marudhanayagam got up from his chair, pushing it back noisily. "You are insulting us. My friend here has offered to buy me—an MLA, no less—lunch at your restaurant. Instead of feeling proud, you are treating your guests shamefully," he shouted.

Rhea shrugged. "If that's the case, it'd be nice if your friend deposited twenty thousand rupees before you both walk into any of the restaurants here."

"What?!" Marudhanayagam's eyes almost popped out of his face. "He's a policeman. Everything's free for him. He..."

Rhea's black eyes blazed in fury. "Why would that be? Doesn't he get a salary for doing his job?"

The MLA was confused. He looked at Rhea first, opening and closing his mouth as he couldn't find the right words to utter before turning to glare at Kamalakannan. "You answer her."

Kamalakannan took one look at her enraged face and clammed up, looking down at his feet.

Rhea looked behind them at Officer Vadivel and said, "Let me introduce Officer Vadivel from the police commissioner's office. Maybe you both will be kind enough to explain yourselves to him." She got up and walked out, leaving the three of them alone.

Her office door opened in barely two minutes and the three men filed out. Vadivel appeared calm, with a benign smile on his face. Kamalakannan looked as if he had been slapped in the face, which is exactly what the politician had done to the man. As for Marudhanayagam, the politician was beyond enraged as he glared at Rhea Bansal. He would get his back on her; he swore to himself even as Officer Vadivel made sure the two men were escorted off the premises.

Jamie was about to step into the reception when he saw a man seeing two men off in a car before a police jeep was brought forth for him. He walked up to the man who was obviously from the police department and said, "Hello, my name's Jamie Scott. I'm an Australian national." He opened his wallet to show the man his ID card.

Vadivel first looked at the identification and then at the man in front of him, impressed despite himself. He nodded to Jamie before saying, "I'm Vadivel from the local police commissioner's office."

"May I ride with you?" asked Jamie politely, keen to know more about the man's visit to Rose Garden International.

"Sure," Officer Vadivel nodded before opening the door with deference to the other man and let him settle down comfortably before walking to the other side and getting in. "Are you here on an assignment, Mr Scott?" he enquired.

"No, I'm on holiday. Was there trouble at the hotel today?" Jamie asked, a dark brow up in query as he scrutinised the officer beside him.

Vadivel sighed. "I'm ashamed to admit it was due to someone from my own department. Inspector Kamalakannan feels that all the hotels owe him free meals just because he's a policeman. He has been banned from Rose Garden International since many months. He has been creating a bit of trouble on and off since then. But those have been averted easily as Ms Bansal filed a complaint with us right at the beginning. Today, he decided to have lunch here along with a politician. He obviously had been hoping he could get away with it because of the high-powered company. But Ms Bansal was too quick for the duo. She called us the moment the security guard informed her the two men had got inside the premises." Vadivel grimaced as he continued, "I only hope she has not created a bigger enemy now."

Jamie couldn't help the feeling of admiration for Rhea. Just as he had thought, she was quick with her decisions. He looked at the other man and said, "Well, I plan to stay back at least a few more weeks right here in Ooty. I can help you by keeping an eye on the hotel and its owner as she's become a good friend."

"Could you do that?" Vadivel felt absolutely relieved. While he admired the woman and knew she was capable of dealing with trouble, Marudhanayagam was dangerous, to say the least. He knew of at least two complaints from which the man had escaped unscathed only because of the influence he wielded with his higher-ups in the government. Both had been from women who had been sexually harassed. It was frustrating to let the man go each time, but that's how it was. The police commissioner was actually hoping to nail the man with some concrete, irrefutable evidence. He now wondered if Jamie Scott would be able to unearth something for them.

Vadivel spoke to the Australian regarding the issue as they chatted all the way to the police commissioner's office. They continued their chat inside before Vadivel introduced Jamie to Commissioner Sakthivel himself. It was a while before Jamie left. Vadivel stepped out of his office to see him off. "Thank you, Jamie." They were on first name terms by now. "It's an honour meeting you. I'm glad there's someone inside the hotel, keeping an eye out." When Jamie nodded, he continued, "Would you like my man to drop you somewhere?"

Jamie shook his head, preferring his independence. "No thanks, mate. I'm good. I'll grab some lunch nearby before doing some more sightseeing." He left with a wave to his new friend.

Jasmine, Anand and Shiva smiled at each other. This was exactly the reason why they held their boss in high esteem. Rhea Bansal was a woman of action. All of them had been around when Inspector Kamalakannan had left the hotel without paying the bill and were aware he was blacklisted. The man was a parasite.

Every night, the hotel fed poor people with the leftover food. Not many people knew of it. But Rhea had been very particular about it right from the start. Whatever food was leftover at night, was packed into containers and stored in deep freezers. The same was warmed up and distributed at three orphanages and two homes which housed the poor the very next morning. Two tempos were kept busy with this job from 7-9 am.

But feeding a policeman and his family for free was just not done. And the man had done his best to brew trouble. The employees were so happy it hadn't worked. Rhea Bansal was clear about her principles and wouldn't bend to blackmail.

What the three of them didn't realise was that Rhea had created a newer and more powerful enemy that afternoon, a man who was a lecher into the bargain.

arudhanayagam maintained a stony silence during the ride back to his office, not wanting the driver to be privy to what had taken place.

Kamalakannan was looking for an opportunity to escape. Halfway to their destination, he gathered his courage in his hands and said, "I can get off here and walk to my office." He tapped the driver to give him instructions. "Stop by the side for a minute and let me off."

"No Dhana, you drive on to the office. I need to talk to KK sir," said the MLA, turning to glare at the policeman, his eyes burning with hatred. He had never been so insulted in his whole life and that too by a woman. And who had been the cause of that? If looks could kill, Kamalakannan would have been a pile of ashes by now.

Kamalakannan wiped his face with a handkerchief, sweating in spite of the extremely cold weather. Marudhanayagam was renowned for his aggressive nature, combined with a strong streak of cruelty, the very reason why the policeman had taken the MLA along with him for the afternoon jaunt to the 5-star hotel. He had so hoped they could get away with a free Chettinadu meal. How he craved it! His empty stomach rumbled loudly, making the MLA turn and look at him with a vindictive smile on his face.

"You are hungry, I suppose," said Marudhanayagam, sarcasm dripping from his voice.

"You must also be hungry, sir," suggested Kamalakannan timidly, refusing to meet the other man's eyes.

"My lunch is awaiting me in my office. Let me see, my wife mentioned something about *kozhi kurma* and *biryani*." He smacked his lips. "As for the 5-star meal, I plan to go there for dinner with my family. Unlike you," he taunted in a savage whisper, "I can afford the meal."

After reaching his office, Marudhanayagam made Kamalakannan wait outside while he finished his meal in a leisurely fashion. *Let the bastard fume! How dare he make a fool of me?!* It was almost an hour before he called Kamalakannan in.

Kamalakannan's stomach protested dreadfully as he caught a whiff of the home-cooked lunch the MLA had just finished. He sat down when the other man pointed to a chair.

"You should have told me KK," he said, his voice mild and silky, belying the fury in his dark eyes. "The hotel has blacklisted you and you didn't bother to tell me. And why did they do that?"

Kamalakannan squirmed, wondering how to get out of the grilling which was coming his way. "They are mad, sir. They..."

"Really?" Marudhanayagam's eyebrows went up at that. "Then why do you think Vadivel rushed to their help?" He wouldn't take the bitch's name. Rhea Bansal didn't know what was coming her way. He would teach her the lesson of her life, one where she would welcome death with open arms.

Kamalakannan didn't know what to say. "Er... I..."

"The truth, KK! And I might let you live," snarled Marudhanayagam.

Kamalakannan blurted out his story, abject fear in his eyes. It was never good to get on the wrong side of a politician, especially one such as the man in front of him.

"So, basically, you were planning to ride on my back. That's not good KK. Get out now. And await your transfer orders to a remote corner of Rajasthan. Then maybe, just maybe, you'll really know what missing your favourite food is," said Marudhanayagam, his smile turning evil. He got up to indicate the meeting was over even as Kamalakannan spluttered, apologising profusely. The MLA pinned the other man with his gaze and spoke softly with just a trace of menace in his voice, "Didn't I just order you to get out?"

Kamalakannan fled!

12

hea came wide awake and turned to look at her bedside clock. It was barely 4 am, but sleep defied her. She got out of her bed, stretching her arms above her head. The first person who came to her mind was Jamie. A small smile quivered on her lips as she thought of the tall and handsome Australian. Never had she imagined she might fall for a westerner. Well, she hadn't really fallen for him yet—at least, nothing she was ready to admit to, even to herself. What if this one too turned out to be a dud?!

Shrugging, Rhea removed an electric blue, one-piece swimsuit from her wardrobe. Removing her nightshirt, she pulled on the swimsuit and, brushing her hair to gather it up into a knot, slipped on a matching swimming cap. Pulling on her track pants and a full-sleeved t-shirt, she wore a knee-length fleece-lined jacket over the lot before she pulled on her socks and shoes. It was too early for guests to go swimming, thought Rhea, glad that she would have the pool to herself.

Jamie entered the building housing the pool ten minutes later. He had been busy exploring Ooty all of yesterday and never got a chance to speak to Rhea. He had tried calling her a couple of times only to find her phone switched off. He was disappointed they hadn't fixed up to go riding this morning. He went to the changing room and pulled off his clothes and stepped under a hot shower before walking out. That's when he noticed a lone figure swimming vigorously. *Isn't it a little too early?* thought Jamie with a small frown. He had so hoped to have the pool to himself so early in the morning.

A wide grin split his face when he saw Rhea swimming in his direction. "Hey," he called out to her as he walked towards the pool.

Rhea stopped midway and tread water, a smile on her face as she brushed a hand over her eyes and stared, unaware that her mouth had fallen open. Jamie looked like a bronzed sculpture come alive, only a pair of brief swimming trunks in black stopping his spectacular body from being gloriously naked. He stepped into the pool, swimming towards her, a wide smile on his face. "Good morning. I was just feeling regretful I hadn't fixed a riding date with you, and here you are." He placed his hands on her slender shoulders, looking down at her gorgeous face and body, his green eyes alive on his rugged face. This was the first time he was seeing her in so brief an attire. With Ooty being cold, the temperatures ranging between twelve and fifteen degrees, everyone tended to wear at least a few layers of clothing which covered them from head to foot. But just now, right in front of him, was Rhea, in a one-piece swimsuit in blue which followed the shape of her hour-glass figure faithfully. Her back was straight and her gorgeous breasts were thrust forward proudly, giving him a peep into her cleavage. The high cut on the thighs underlined the shape of her hips and long legs. His heart picked up tempo as he drank in her magnificent body, tearing his eyes away from it with an effort before looking into her eyes.

Rhea felt her shoulders tingle in reaction to his touch, goose bumps dancing all over her skin even as blood rushed to her cheeks. "Hey," she greeted in a choked whisper, looking up at him. Without being aware of what she was doing, she stepped on Jamie's feet, her hands on his muscular shoulders, to reach up and brush her lips against his, a small sigh escaping inadvertently from her chest.

Jamie's breath caught in his throat when he felt the touch of her lips, soft like a butterfly's wings against his mouth. He raised a hand to cup her cheek, holding her head steady as he pressed his mouth to hers in a soft kiss.

Raising his head, he looked down at her face, her eyes shut tightly, long, curling eyelashes brushing against her blushing cheeks. He let go of her with reluctance, saying, "Race you to the other end," before swimming away swiftly.

A startled Rhea opened her eyes to see him already halfway down the pool and called out, "That's cheating! I wasn't ready. Let's start again."

They did twenty laps up and down the pool, giving stiff competition to each other. Though he was taller than her, Jamie had to admit she was tenacious and an extremely strong swimmer. He grinned to himself. She sure was competitive and meant to win.

"I concede defeat. You won twelve times while I got there first only eight times," he winked at her.

Rhea gave him a wide smile and declared, "You aren't a bad swimmer."

Jamie burst out laughing. And they called him a swimming champ back home.

They got out by silent mutual consent and went their separate ways to the changing rooms before meeting once again near the pool. "What? You are on holiday?" asked Jamie, eyeing her casual clothes.

"I start at ten today. I'm planning to have a huge breakfast. Want to join me?" She looked at him with her dark gaze, admiring what she saw. He was wearing jeans and a full t-shirt of teal blue which had a hood. His dark blond locks were brushed back neatly away from his broad forehead. The dark gold fuzz on his cheeks underlined his masculinity, while his jade green eyes sparkled with life.

"Would love to! What were you thinking of having?"

"Have you tasted a typical South Indian breakfast? *Idli, vadai, dosai* and the whole works?"

Jamie thought of his meals over the past few days and said, "I don't think so. Is that vegetarian? I had only non-veg meals except for the lunch I had at Coonoor."

"Yeah, it's vegetarian. You're in for a treat then. Come on, let's go." She tucked her hand into the crook of his elbow and walked out of the building towards Bugatti, the coffee shop which served both South Indian as well as Continental fare round the clock.

There was a lavish breakfast buffet spread, set against two adjacent walls with no less than forty dishes. They took two plates and walked from one end to the other, checking out what was on offer.

Jamie piled his plate with every item she pointed at. "I'm hungry enough to eat a horse. That was a tough race you gave me at the pool."

Rhea laughed, sitting down in the chair he pulled out for her. "Glad to know." She gestured to a waiter who walked over.

"Good morning, ma'am, sir," greeted Sriram, smiling at them.

"Good morning, Sriram. Could you bring us some filter coffee please?"

"Sure ma'am," said Sriram, taking an about turn to get the coffee.

"I must say that the service is excellent as is the food," said Jamie, tucking into his meal heartily. "This is shaped like a doughnut and is deep fried too," he said, forking a piece of *vadai* into his mouth. "Mmm... yummy. It doesn't taste anything like a doughnut though. I like it. What's it made of?"

"Black gram soaked over a few hours and ground to a pulp. It's shaped and deep fried to make crispy *vadai*. You soak it in *sambar*," she demonstrated it to him, "and eat it; or with any of these three chutneys. They add to the flavour."

Jamie nodded, trying out the variety of chutneys. "Delicious."

They didn't talk much as they ate their way through two more helpings from the buffet before the restaurant became crowded with other guests.

"And where are you off to today?" asked Rhea. She walked towards the back entrance of the restaurant as it was the closest to her home.

"House hunting."

"Huh!" Her eyes went wide as she stopped to stare at him. "You were serious about staying back in Ooty. For how long?"

"Maybe a couple of months," he shrugged.

Rhea was secretly thrilled to hear that. Suddenly coming to a decision, she said, "Come along with me."

Jamie went with her to her home. Rhea opened the door and shut it the moment they got in from the cold. The house was warm and snug. She turned to him and said, "Since it's only for a couple of months, would you like to be a paying guest in my home? It's large and only I live here. If you go searching outside, you might get fleeced as they come up with exorbitant rents for short stays..."

Jamie stepped forward to place his index against her lips, effectively stopping her from speaking further. "You don't have to sell the idea to me. I'm sold already," he grinned. "It'd be awesome if I could get paying guest accommodation in this palatial home which reeks of history."

Rhea stared at him, her lips tingling at his touch. She must be mad to invite him to spend two long months in her home. But then, she'd be a fool to let go of this opportunity to get to know him better. Her tongue came out to lick her suddenly dry lips, inadvertently brushing against his finger.

"Rhea..." Jamie looked deeply into her startled black gaze, his heart picking up beat. That quick swipe of her tongue against his finger had made him go hard.

"I..." Rhea's eyelashes fluttered against her cheeks as she brought her gaze down to the level of his chest, unable to meet the heat in his gaze. Her stomach was in knots as tension gathered in her mid-section.

Jamie brushed his finger over her lips, tracing their shape. "You look beautiful," he said in a whisper before bending down to claim her quivering lips in a deep kiss.

hea melted in Jamie's arms, hanging on to his shoulders for support. But for his arms which had curved around her slim waist, she would have sunk to the floor, her legs having gone weak and rubbery. She opened her lips to let his tongue in and felt her heart hammer against her chest as he explored her mouth thoroughly, making sounds of appreciation in his throat which aroused her to fever pitch.

It was a while before they came up for air and Rhea buried her face against his chest. So that was how a kiss felt! It was explosive, mind blowing! She took deep breaths to calm down her heart but it simply refused to listen.

But Rhea being Rhea, she was keen to check out Jamie's mouth, the same way he had explored hers. Raising her head from his chest, she locked her arms around his neck, pulling his head down. She ran a damp tongue over the seam of his lips, seeking entry.

Becoming aware of what she was doing, Jamie smiled against her mouth, before drawing her tongue within. He held her close, his body growing harder still as she swept her tongue inside the cavern of his mouth, a tad hesitant at first.

Rhea grew bolder as she relished the sensations which played havoc with her nervous system. He tasted so good and all male. Drunk on it, she tangled her tongue with his, wanting more.

Jamie lifted his head to gaze down at the blissful expression on her face and suddenly felt his hammering heart grow steady, as if a deep calm had settled down after a storm. Dazed, he wondered if this is what falling in love was all about. It was as if... as if his heart knew it had met its mate and had moved into a state of idyllic joy.

He pressed his lips gently over her left eye, absorbing the peace which stole into his body, mind and soul. He smiled as her lashes fluttered against his lips before tracing a path down her temple to her ear. He nuzzled her, brushing his tongue against the rapidly beating pulse below her ear, making her moan.

"Rhea..." Jamie whispered softly into her ear as he buried his face against the crook of her neck.

Rhea felt shaken, her emotions going for a toss as she slowly but surely lost control over herself—both her body and mind. And that was something she couldn't allow. With a jerk, she pulled out of Jamie's arms, turning away, tucking a strand of hair nervously behind her ear. Taking deep breaths, she strived to bring a semblance of calm to her stormy feelings.

Jamie's kisses were amazing, till the point when she began to feel as if she was being tossed about like a piece of flotsam in the middle of a raging river. Loss of control was something she couldn't deal with. If that is what Jamie's lovemaking was going to do to her, Rhea could do without it in her life.

Jamie looked at Rhea as she stood away from him, facing the other way, her slender body trembling. His smile morphed into a grin as he understood the turmoil seething within her. The strong lady liked to be in charge. It was up to him to convince her it wasn't he who was trying to control her but her own needs and hormones. He wondered if even then she would let herself go. It promised to be fun—him discovering the many layers which were Rhea, along with her—*if* she would let them actually do it, that is.

"Will you show me your home?" asked Jamie as if nothing had happened.

Rhea turned to him in a flash, her black eyes turbulent. He looked so bloody cool. The kisses which had had an earth-shattering effect on her didn't seem to have affected him at all. But for all she knew, he probably kissed women—in the plural—all the time. For a moment Rhea was ready to commit murder before she took a deep breath and brought her fuming temper under wraps.

"Of course," she said, turning to the door on the right, her face unsmiling.

Jamie's grin became wider as he followed her, remaining a couple of steps behind, his gaze travelling at leisure over her back, taking its time to follow the gentle sway of her hips as he savoured the untrammelled view.

They walked down a narrow corridor which had a door on either side. She opened the one on the left to show him a large bedroom which was completely furnished with a four-poster bed, a wardrobe and a dressing table. The wall opposite the door was fitted with ceiling-to-floor windows while the one on the right sported French windows which led into the garden. Jamie could see the stables and the building which housed the Bugatti restaurant from there. The room had an attached bathroom with modern fittings.

"The door on the other side is a mirror image of this one. You can choose either of the two, whichever you prefer," said Rhea, still feeling irritated and refusing to look at him.

"This is perfect," said Jamie. "I hope you'll let me share your kitchen."

She looked at him, appearing surprised. "Do you plan to cook?"

Jamie shrugged. "I need to eat, so I suppose I'll cook. Why?"

"Oh. I didn't think. Sorry." There was a time when Rhea had done a lot of cooking, but not any longer. It was one of those skills which she had wanted to learn in order to be self-sufficient, but didn't really use nowadays. "Why not? Come along." She took him back the way they had come, into the living room and then turned right, their path leading them further back into the house.

They entered a large and cavernous space which housed a modern kitchen unit, complete with an oven, microwave and fridge on the left, and a circular dining table and chairs to accommodate four on the right. Rhea swept her arm around. "Here you go. It's all yours, though I must warn you that you'll need to stock up on groceries."

"This is exactly what I need," said Jamie, opening and shutting cupboards and drawers, taking note of the utensils and crockery. While the refrigerator was switched on, there were only a few bottles of soft drinks and wine in it. "Will you mind if I cook meat here? Or is it strictly vegetarian?"

Rhea stared at him with a look of amazement. "Of course not! Go ahead and make whatever you want."

"And the rent? You'll need an advance too."

"Huh!" Rhea had suggested he stay here only because she wanted to get to know him better and had not thought beyond that point. Now she wondered if she had done the right thing. Well, she would just have to keep her distance; it was as simple as that. With a mental shrug, she said, "Anything you want to give. I haven't really thought about it," she said disinterestedly.

With an intention to provoke her out of her apathy, Jamie said, "I don't want your charity," his tongue firmly in his cheek.

A bright flame lit up in her black eyes as Rhea glared at him. "I'm not offering you charity. Okay, I'll find out what the market rate is and will charge you the same. You can give me two months' rent wholly in advance. Do you plan to finish your stay at the hotel or cancel the rest of it and move in here immediately?" He still had six days to go from his earlier booking.

Jamie hid his smile with difficulty. "I'll move here after I'm done with my stay at your hotel. I quite like it there, especially the heated swimming pool and the complimentary breakfast."

"Okay," said Rhea abruptly. "Since it's only going to be two months, I'm not too keen on a legal contract and all those formalities, unless you insist on it. What do you think?"

"I'm good. I don't think you can bodily throw me out even if you want to," he shrugged, his face straight. "So, it works for me."

"Don't be too sure," muttered Rhea, giving him a murderous glance before turning away to walk into the living room.

Jamie shook with silent laughter. Life promised to be such fun with Rhea!

14

Two weeks had gone by since Jamie had moved into Rhea's cottage, after paying her twenty thousand rupees in advance against two months' rent. They had verbally agreed she would take care of the electricity, water and gas bills while he would bring the grocery to provide for his meals. The transition from hotel to home had been without incident and managed to lull Rhea into a state of calm. She was confident now that her life was back within her control.

Jamie taught himself to make filter coffee the South Indian way and greeted her every morning with a fresh cup. Otherwise, he was extremely careful not to step into Rhea's space. He was so reminded of the butterfly which he had held in his small hands as a child. It had been so desperate for freedom that he let it go after a few seconds, only to have it turn around and settle down on his open palm, much to his joy. Would Rhea become his, like the butterfly? The only way to find out was to let her go—be, in this case.

He was regularly in touch with Officer Vadivel from the police commissioner's office. Between the two of them, they continued to keep track of MLA Marudhanayagam's movements. Jamie also spent at least a couple of hours at the hotel reception befriending the front office staff, especially Shiva. He was so glad Rhea had insisted he should feel free to use the pool at his convenience. And he did go riding from time to time. He had even taken up a minor project locally, designing the home of a local farmer.

Somasekhar had been living in an old dilapidated cottage all his life, patching up the roof now and again when something went wrong. He had been working hard and saving money for years. Now that his three children were older and were of marriageable age, they insisted that they build a new family home with four independent suites along with a common kitchen. The construction was almost finished while they had been on the lookout for someone to help with the interiors. That's when their neighbour Vadivel had introduced his new interior designer friend to them.

Sathya, Prakash and Pavithra were impressed by Jamie Scott's projects when they checked them out on his website. "If he is a white man from Australia, he might charge too much, Vadivel. Have you considered that?" asked Somasekhar, a worried frown on his face. He had money, loads of it. But he liked to keep a tight hold on his purse strings.

Vadivel laughed. "Come on Uncle, you can afford it. You build a house maybe once in a lifetime. Why don't you make a grand affair out of it?" He continued when Somasekhar's daughter and sons nodded their heads vigorously, "Though I don't think you should worry on that count. Jamie is here on holiday, but doesn't like being idle. He makes a lot of money from his corporate clients. Maybe he won't charge as much for a private house."

In the end, Somasekhar found out to his joy, that Jamie Scott's consulting fees were far lesser than some of the local designers. He was absolutely impressed by the Australian's warm attitude. While he spoke only a few sentences of English, his children conversed comfortably with Jamie, explaining their requirements.

"I think we should use as many local materials as possible, for two reasons. They can be replaced in case of damage at the least cost. For another, the wear and tear will be less as the materials will thrive better in local weather conditions without too much maintenance. The best part of the deal will be that you can source them at a reasonable cost with minimal effort," said Jamie.

Somasekhar was floored by this logic. While his children had been thinking in the lines of Italian marble and Belgium glass, the interior designer had convinced them so easily with his reasoning.

"And you don't need to worry about the finish. I'll ensure what I design is delivered to the T. What I'll do is conduct a study of your home and create two different ideas. You can all check them out and tell me if either of those works for you. What say?"

Sathya said, "Yes," before his father could say anything. "That would be perfect. About the materials..."

"I have been checking out Ooty for different things, more out of interest than anything else," smiled Jamie. "I'll give you the design along with the raw materials which I plan to use, my cost and the cost of setting everything up; though I'll need to find out what the locals charge for the actual decoration work."

"I know just the person for that," said Prakash. "I'll find out the cost and time involved and get back to you regarding that."

"Perfect," said Jamie, getting up from his chair. "Let me get back to you with the promised designs in three days. I'll come in the daylight tomorrow to see your new home. Will that be convenient?"

"Of course," said Sathya. "You are welcome, Mr Scott."

"Call me Jamie," he smiled, shaking the younger man's hand.

Somasekhar's wife Padmaja, who had been hovering in the background throughout the discussion, gave Jamie a winning smile even if she hadn't understood a single word of the conversation flowing around her. All she could see was that her husband and three children were happy, which was more than enough for her. She told her husband to invite the interior designer to stay back for dinner. Jamie politely refused, claiming a prior appointment. He left with a promise to have breakfast at their home the next morning.

"Thanks mate," he bumped a fist with Vadivel's before they got into the latter's car. "I'm delighted to have something to work on during my stay here. And designing a home in a strange environment is surely a challenge."

Vadivel nodded, smiling. "No matter. I'm glad to be of help. And by the way, keep a look out for any new employee at Rose Garden International. I heard a rumour that the MLA is trying to get his man inside."

Jamie frowned even as he nodded. "I wonder what he plans to achieve."

"The man's a womaniser through and through. And take my word for it that he'll never forgive Rhea Bansal for the insult he suffered the other day during his visit to the hotel."

"How powerful is he? Is his reach very high?" asked Jamie.

"High enough to have had Inspector KK transferred to a remote village in Rajasthan within a week of their hotel visit." Vadivel shrugged. "I know the man had been begging for it, but that also shows how dangerous Marudhanayagam can be when he's crossed."

"It's a good thing I'm living in Rhea's house these days as her PG," grinned Jamie.

"Which is truly a stroke of luck," said Vadivel, giving the other man a curious look. While they had got rather close, he didn't want to ask the other man any personal questions as he wondered about his relationship with Rhea Bansal. He probably was only a paying guest just as he had mentioned.

Vadivel let Jamie off near the hotel's reception before taking off to his home.

15

Jamie woke up suddenly in the middle of the night to see that it was almost one am. He wondered what had disturbed him when he heard it again—the noise which had woken him up in the first place; it sounded like someone crashing into furniture and swearing virulently in a strange language. Pulling on a pair of shorts over his naked body, he rushed into the living room and switched on the light to see Rhea sprawled across the couch on her front, one leg and one arm hanging outside. She was fully clothed. What the hell!

"Rhea," he called out, rushing to her to check if she was hurt.

"Jhamieeee..." she slurred, turning on her back when he tried to lift her into a more comfortable position. "Whaddarudoing?"

"Are you drunk?" he asked, hiding a smile. She looked cute, her face flushed and her hair all over the place.

"I ashked..." Rhea raised a palm in front of her as if asking for a time-out and repeated, "I ashked fusht. You anshwer me." She gave him a silly grin.

"What?" Jamie lifted her up in his arms, planning to take her to her room.

"Whaddarudoing? Put me down, Jhamieeee. Lishten..."

"Shh, keep quiet, will you? You're no lightweight you know! Let me get you to your bed," said Jamie cheekily. He had no trouble carrying her except for his heart kicking wildly even as it pumped extra blood to his lower body.

"I won't," said Rhea, glaring at him or at least trying to, only her hair kept getting in the way. Her left arm was hanging down the side while her right was sandwiched between his body and hers.

Jamie let her slide down his body and made her stand, holding her upright with his left arm while he pulled back the cover on her bed with his right. He lifted her again to place her in the middle of the bed, before going to the end of the bed to pull her knee length boots off.

Rhea struggled wildly, kicking. "I don't wanna shleep," she told him firmly, pushing her hair out of her eyes to glare at him.

"Wild cat," said Jamie, managing to remove both the boots before climbing on the bed to sit at her side. "What do you want to do then?"

"Kish you," said Rhea, pulling him down close to her body, placing her lips on his bare chest. She turned her head and pressed an ear to the region of his heart and exclaimed, "Are you wohkay Jhamieee?" Her eyes were wide as she looked up at his face. "Your heart ish beating likega drum. It'sh so loud that my head ish hurding." She flopped on his chest, fast asleep the next second, snoring gently.

Jamie groaned loudly; hugging Rhea close to his chest. The woman was going to lead him a fine dance for sure. He held her for about ten minutes and then gently settled her down on the bed before walking away quietly to spend a sleepless night in his room.

Rhea woke up the next morning with a mild headache and wondered why she was sleeping with all her clothes on. And how had she got into bed? She frowned, trying to recall the events of the night. She had had a couple of drinks with some friends who had come over for dinner. It had been late when she got home. She remembered she had knocked her knee against a table and… had she sworn? She must have, as she vaguely recalled swearing in Hindi. What had happened after that? Rhea shook her head, failing to recall. She clutched her head immediately. Moving her head had been a mistake as it made it hurt more. She got up from the bed when she heard a knock on the door. Jamie had never come to this side of her home from the time he moved in a couple of weeks ago. Rhea opened the door to see him standing outside with a tray in his hand.

"Good morning," he greeted her cheerfully, "This is green tea with lemon and honey. Drink it up and your hangover will be gone in a jiffy."

Rhea frowned up at him, looking into his eyes, refusing to look at all the bare skin as he was clad only in shorts. "And why do you think I might have a hangover?" she asked.

Jamie walked in to place the tray on the table by her bedside. "Do you recall how you got into your bed last night?" he asked, a mischievous glint in his green eyes. He was wide awake despite tossing and turning on his bed most of the night.

Rhea's frown deepened. What did he know which she didn't? "Why?"

"Drink this Rhea, before it turns cold," said Jamie, lifting the glass and handing it to her.

She obeyed him, without realising what she was doing. Feeling better almost immediately, she pinned him with her black gaze to ask, "What happened last night?"

"What?" Jamie asked, pretending to be surprised, "You mean you don't know?"

Rhea got a mite worried. Why the hell was he looking so smug? To add to the already confounding thoughts in her head, Jamie stood before her in only a pair of shorts, looking good enough to eat. She was having a tough time not staring at his muscular body which didn't have a spare ounce of flesh.

The blood pounded in her head for a different reason now as she became completely aware of him. But what the hell! She had seen him wearing less when they went swimming! All that raw masculinity was getting to her and she felt such an intense need to explore his body. While she couldn't recall how she had got into bed, she was confident nothing untoward must have happened as she was still in the same clothes she had been wearing when she went out for dinner last evening. He hadn't even tried to undress her. A deep sigh issued from within her. Wasn't he interested in her anymore? After... Rhea frowned, trying to recall when was the last time they had kissed. It was on the day she had shown him her home. And that was some three weeks ago. What the fuck!

Rhea turned away, frustrated.

Jamie watched her, keeping his distance. He knew she wouldn't appreciate it if he tried to kiss her, let alone make love to her. The decision needed to be hers. While the wait was exasperating, he knew it was the only way to win her confidence.

"You fell asleep on the couch in the living room. I brought you here and put you to bed," said Jamie, his voice gentle.

She turned to look at him with turbulent black eyes. "Did you have to carry me?"

Jamie nodded. "Yep."

She walked up to him and whispered, "Sorry to have put you to so much trouble. I must've been so heavy to lift. Tch!"

He traced a velvet cheek with his forefinger, unable to resist. "It was no trouble."

Rhea shut her eyes; her feelings acute as she felt his touch against her cheek. What would he do if she responded in kind? There was only one way to find out. Turning her head, she kissed his finger, holding his hand against her face. "Jamie..." Rhea whispered and was rewarded for her efforts when two strong arms gathered her close to his body. Shuddering, she buried her face in his massive chest, rubbing her face against the rough, golden curls like a little kitten, unaware of the small moans emanating from her throat.

Jamie held her close, rubbing his chin against the top of her head, a large hand caressing her back. It wasn't easy waiting for her to take the initiative when all he wanted to do was to throw her on the bed and make her his.

Rhea moved away to look up at him. His eyes were shut and she was fascinated by the long gold-tipped eyelashes which fell on his lean cheeks. Going on tiptoe, she kissed a corner of his lips. So, what if he hadn't bothered to kiss her? She was pretty capable of doing the honours. Her tongue peeped out to trace the shape of his mouth.

Jamie grinned to himself. It looked like the butterfly had finally landed on his palm. He let her explore his lips for a few moments before he thrust his tongue into her mouth, kissing her deeply. His hands caressed her back, moving down to her shapely bottom, bringing her body close to his aroused one.

Rhea gasped when she felt his erection against her stomach. What had she unleashed?! Panic struck her as she struggled in his arms.

Jamie refused to let go as he growled, "Calm down Rhea. I'm not going to rape you. I won't do anything which you don't want me to do. Do you get me?" He looked at her intensely with glowing green eyes, willing her to understand.

Rhea stopped struggling, going still in his arms. "I... I don't know what got into me. I'm sorry," she said in a whisper.

He kissed her again, briefly. "You do realise there's something going on between us?"

Rhea gave him a small nod, her eyes wary.

"Which is why I have extended my stay in Ooty. Otherwise, I'd have left long ago," he continued to talk to her softly.

"But..."

Jamie placed a finger over her quivering lips. "We'll go along at the pace you set. Would you like that? I've been craving to kiss you these past few weeks," he declared truthfully. "But I felt you weren't all that keen." His left eyebrow went up questioningly.

Rhea looked at him in wonder, her black gaze clinging to his. Jamie had stayed back in Ooty because of her. She pressed closer to his body, feeling secure in his arms, wrapping her own around his waist. "I was scared," she continued to speak in a whisper. "Like I told you before, my relationships with men haven't been the best in the world."

What relationships?! He could have sworn she was a virgin. She even kissed like one. But now wasn't the time to ask. "Will you kiss me now?" he invited mischievously, winking at her when her head came up at his question.

Her gaze turned naughty as she eyed his mouth as one would eye a favourite dessert. "Would love to," she said, pressing her lips to his mouth before pushing her tongue within. Rhea felt like a kid at a candy store as Jamie let her have her way with him, simply responding to her overtures, only giving and not taking.

Rhea giggled when they came up for air. "Tell me the truth, how bad was it?"

"What?" asked Jamie, a dazed look in his eyes which wiped the smile from her face, "What was bad?"

"You liked my kiss?" she asked, her eyes wide in amazement which soon turned to disappointment when Jamie shook his head. "You didn't?" Her face fell.

"No," whispered Jamie in her ear, "I adored it."

Rhea buried her face in his chest and wept.

Hugging her close to his person, Jamie didn't care he was late for his breakfast appointment. Rhea was the most important person in his life right now.

To Jamie, it was like when he was in his early teens. He had a girlfriend he held hands with, necked with and kissed some times. Even though the kisses were intense, they never went beyond that. He was surprised at himself at times, at the kind of control he wielded over his libido. But then, he was ready to go to any length to earn Rhea's trust. Hopefully love would follow.

Rhea floated in a dream world these days. She had a boyfriend who pandered to her every whim. While she felt the intense heat of his green gaze many a time, he never asked for more than what she was ready to give. She was truly lucky and she appreciated that, doing her best to spend as much time as possible with him despite her hectic schedule.

"My brother Rohit's throwing a party this Friday," she said, seated comfortably on Jamie's lap in her living room as they shared a glass of toddy. She turned up to look at his face. "Will you go with me?"

"Will that be in Mumbai?" asked Jamie, his eyes roving over her face before settling on her lips. "Give me a kiss and I'll think about it."

Rhea punched his arm with a fist before obliging him. After kissing him passionately, she moved away to ask, "Will you go with me now?"

"I'm thinking," he insisted, his chest rumbling with laughter, before he buried his face in the crook of her neck. "I'll go to the end of the earth with you, Rhea."

"There you go again! Why do you want to make me cry?" asked Rhea, her voice choked.

"Of course, I don't want you to do that. I only said what I meant. So, when do you want to leave?"

And it was as simple as that.

They left on Friday afternoon, when a car from the hotel dropped them at the hotel's private helipad. "Are we travelling by that beast?" asked Jamie, eyeing the sleek black machine.

Rhea nodded, "Yeah, till Coimbatore airport. We'll take a flight from there."

Jamie nodded, watching Rhea as she unlocked the door. He lifted her to help her into the copter after placing their luggage inside. "Not from here Jamie. I'll climb in from the other side."

He stared at her, a slow grin building on his face. "Don't tell me you're the pilot?"

"What's so funny about that?" she growled at him, a scowl on her face.

Jamie stretched a hand to wipe out the frown on her forehead before pulling her into his arms. "Why are you defensive? I'm just surprised and *impressed*," he stressed on the word, "with the varied skills you possess. You're a superwoman."

Mollified, Rhea apologised sweetly before giving him an intense kiss.

"I don't mind if you get angry as often as you want to, if that's how we're going to make up," said Jamie, winking at her.

Rhea poked her tongue at him before walking to the other side and climbing inside the copter. The ride was uneventful and they reached the airport in twenty-five minutes.

It was evening when they met Rhea's younger brother Ritvik at the Mumbai airport. Travelling from Udaipur, he had arrived at the airport half an hour earlier.

Rhea hugged Ritvik, offering her cheek for his kiss. "Is it possible that you've grown taller?" she teased, looking at her handsome brother.

"Very funny," he said, eyeing the tall Australian beside her.

"This is Jamie Scott from Australia. He's come to Ooty for a holiday." Turning to Jamie, Rhea said, "Ritvik Bansal, my younger brother."

The two men eyed each other, taking an instant liking to one another as they shook hands warmly.

"So is my sis making you run around in circles yet?" asked Ritvik, a mischievous grin on his face.

"Ritvik!" Rhea gave him a killing look even as Jamie guffawed loudly.

"Totally," said Jamie, winking at the other man.

"Men!" Rhea fumed, picking her suitcase from the baggage carousel before walking towards the exit in a huff.

"Sweetheart!" said Jamie's voice in her ear as his hand closed over her shoulder. "Do you wanna make up?"

She took one look at his face and burst out laughing, shaking her head. "Later on, I promise. PDA is frowned upon in India."

"Will you give me a couple of minutes to collect my baggage or are you going to leave me stranded here at the airport?" he asked, tongue-in-cheek.

Rhea laughed some more before pressing a brief kiss on his cheek, unable to stop herself.

Ritvik looked dazed as he turned his head from one to the other. Rhea must be in love with Jamie! He had never seen his sister appear so light-hearted, ever.

Rhea caught her brother's gaze on her face and blushed fierily.

Although Jamie chatted on and off with Rhea's family, he was more of an observer than a participant at Rohit Bansal's party. He was totally impressed with the opulence of Simha International. It was classy, to say the least. He noticed that all the three Bansal siblings looked more like their father than their diminutive mother. It was obvious Rohit was in love with Tasha and she returned his feelings in equal measure. A marriage seemed to be on the cards soon.

Jamie smiled when he saw Rhea's older brother looking in his direction. "I hope you like the food, Jamie. Or would you prefer something different?" asked Rohit, walking up to him.

"Everything's delicious, mate. I must compliment you on the authenticity of the Japanese food," said Jamie. "Do you have a local chef or...?"

Rohit smiled, pleased. "You got that right. Not a local chef. Akimoto Misaki comes from Japan."

"Aah! No wonder. Amazing hotel you have here. I'm looking forward to the tour you promised me."

"Of course. You've been in Ooty long?" asked Rohit, ever protective of his sister as he wondered what Jamie meant to her.

"A few weeks."

"It must be pretty cold there nowadays."

"Very cold and beautiful. I'm falling more in love with the place each day."

Rohit chatted with Jamie for a few more minutes before moving on, unable to garner much information from him.

It was almost two in the morning when the party broke up. They were all staying over at Rohit's penthouse which had four bedrooms.

Everyone had settled down for the night, after Rohit dropped Tasha at her apartment. Rhea knocked on Rohit's door and walked in, confident he would still be awake.

"Rhea, come on in. I was hoping you would drop by," said Rohit, getting up to give her a hug and pulling her down to sit next to him on the bed. "So, what's up?" he asked, a dark brow up in query. "Jamie's more than a friend," he declared in the next breath.

Rhea turned red. "Do you think so? I'm not really sure, Rohit. Yeah, he's become a close friend, actually my first boyfriend," she grinned impishly. "What do you think of him?"

"Jamie seems decent enough. I want you to be happy, Rhea. Tell me, does he have feelings for you?"

Rhea nodded. "Yes!"

Rohit hugged his sister, pressing his cheek to her head. "I hope things work out for you both. But promise me you'll tell me if he creates any kind of trouble. I'll break his bones." While his tone was teasing, Rohit was deadly serious. The incident with Nayan had affected him terribly.

"If something goes wrong, it's my bones which would need breaking, Rohit. Jamie's too good for me," stated Rhea quietly. Speaking to her brother helped as the truth of her own words hit her hard.

Rohit turned to look at her and grinned. "I think you're falling for him."

Rhea nodded. "In a big way."

"Are you sleeping with him?" asked Rohit bluntly.

"Am I asking you about Tasha?" Rhea glared at him. "Don't come all big brother on me!"

"I've been in a relationship with Tasha for three years. I would have told you if you had asked," said Rohit, his right eyebrow up as he still waited for her answer.

Rhea gave him a sly look. "Oh really! Not when your relationship was new, you wouldn't have."

"So, you *are* sleeping with him," he declared.

"Rohit! I'm going to be thirty-one on my upcoming birthday. What kind of a question is that?" Rhea glowered at him some more.

"Oh yeah, I know. And running your own hotel very successfully too. Blah, blah and blah. How does it stop you from being my kid sister?"

Rhea rolled her eyes. "And no, I'm not sleeping with Jamie," she said.

Rohit gave her a curious look. "Are you sure the man's not impotent?" he asked, grinning widely.

Rhea hit him with a pillow, unable to stop the colour which rushed to her face. She knew for sure Jamie was anything but that. "There's no pleasing you."

"So, is he staying at Rose Garden?"

Rhea nodded. "Not the hotel, but the cottage."

"What?! He's living in your cottage?" Rohit was amazed. Rhea wouldn't let anyone except her family in. Her home was sacrosanct. She must hold Jamie in extremely high regard if he was allowed to live there. He crossed his fingers surreptitiously, wishing his sister a wonderful future.

They chatted for a long time, catching up on things, before Rhea went back to her room after four am.

Ritvik turned to look at Jamie as the Australian followed him to the room they were sharing. "Would you rather I get out and send Rhea in?"

"Not if you want me to die of frustration," declared Jamie, grinning.

"Oh! Then she's really running you around in circles."

"I'm not complaining. My life's good, mate." Jamie shrugged.

"Are you up for sainthood?" asked Ritvik, a mischievous look in his black eyes which so reminded Jamie of Rhea.

"Just because I'm wise?" asked Jamie.

Ritvik laughed. "I think you are." He shook his head, dazed. "You really understand Rhea I think."

Jamie nodded with a smile on his face. "To some extent, yeah. I'd like a few minutes alone with the jerks who have hurt her." His smile disappeared when he said that, the green gaze turning deadly.

Ritvik was so happy to know Rhea had a champion in Jamie. "Do you want to know what happened?"

Jamie had stripped down to his boxers by now and settled back on his bed, as had Ritvik. "You bet! Would you tell me?"

"It's happened to her twice, guys treating her badly. One of them was Rohit's college friend. She was attracted to Nayan, but he turned out to be an asshole, trying to force himself on her." Ritvik paused, his voice choking. He'd been a little over fourteen when it happened and had been totally shaken.

Jamie's face had gone red even as his eyes sparked angrily. He didn't utter a word, waiting for Ritvik to continue.

"Well, he had never met the likes of Rhea in his life," said Ritvik, giving a small smile as he recalled what had happened. "She bit him hard when he tried to kiss her and shoved her knee up his crotch. I am sure she made him dysfunctional for a long time." Ritvik was grinning now.

Jamie smiled, though the smile didn't quite reach his eyes. He was feeling too raw and angry on Rhea's behalf.

"And then Rhea decided to take self-defence classes. My parents and Rohit were all for it. She's a black belt in Taekwondo."

"Did the man get away with what he did? Didn't Rohit give him his due?"

"Not just Rohit but Pappa and I also gave him more than what he deserved. He ran away, never to be seen again."

Jamie nodded, calming down a bit, his heart going out to the young Rhea. "How old was Rhea then?"

Ritvik squinted his eyes, thinking hard. "A couple of months over seventeen, if I remember right."

I will make her forget that bastard, swore Jamie to himself. "And the other guy?"

"Sujit was her boss when she worked at a hotel in Bangalore. She had thought highly of him, only to change her opinion when she realised that he believed a woman's place was in the kitchen and bedroom; and in that order."

Jamie burst out laughing. "I'm dying to know how she dealt with him."

Ritvik laughed along with Jamie now. "I'll let her tell you the story. I'm sure it'll be way more fun that way."

17

On returning to Ooty, Jamie got busy completing the designing project he had taken up for the farming family. He hired the firm of decorators known to Prakash, but only after meeting up with three different contractors. He was clear of getting a competitive rate. They got the work underway while he made it a point to visit the site every day, sometimes even twice when necessary.

"Where do you go every day?" asked Rhea curiously when he let himself into the cottage late one evening.

"Just to check on the project I'm working on. What are you drinking?" he asked, looking at her glass.

"Some dark rum and cola. It's too bloody cold outside."

"Did you just get in?" he asked, going to the bar to get a brandy and soda for himself.

"Yeah. I went riding after two days. Poor Gulliver was damn upset with me," she shrugged.

Jamie sat next to her and wrapped his arms around her, pressing her face into his shoulder. "Comfy?" he asked, rubbing his chin over the top of her head.

Rhea moved to sit in his lap, pushing her arms into his leather jacket to hug him around the middle. "Yeah, now I am."

Jamie grinned, happy to cuddle her. In barely a few minutes, it became hot and he removed his jacket. By now, Rhea was toast warm and was ready to shed hers too. She didn't want to drink the rum any more. "Jamie?" She looked up into his handsome face, enthralled by the golden fuzz on his face. She raised a hand to caress his cheek, loving the rough texture.

He gave her his complete attention, studying the expressions flitting across her beautiful face. "Hmm."

"Will you kiss me?"

Jamie bent his head to place his lips on her cheek, his breath teasing the tendrils of hair dancing around her face. He drew a line with his mouth down to her lips, touching a corner with his tongue.

Rhea's heartbeat picked up tempo as she turned restlessly in his arms. He was taking his own sweet damn time to kiss her. Impatient, she turned her head to capture his lips with her own, just as Jamie knew she would. Only he took over from there and explored her mouth thoroughly. "You taste so good," he said, raising his head to look down at her red face as she fought hard to pace out her breathing.

"As do you," said Rhea. She traced the pulse at his throat with a forefinger, fascinated by the speed at which it was beating. So, he wasn't immune to her proximity, even though his breathing appeared normal. She became excited when she replaced her finger with her lips, flicking a warm tongue over the pulse.

"Rhea..." groaned Jamie, crushing her in his arms.

"I'm sorry. You don't like it? I..."

Jamie shook his head vigorously. "I like it too much."

Growing bolder, she opened the buttons on his shirt to press feather-light kisses on his chest. Fascinated by a flat golden nipple, she dragged her wet tongue over it, savouring the taste, and was startled when she felt Jamie's hand in her hair, pushing her head closer to his body.

Silence reigned in the living room for a long time as Rhea explored his muscular chest with her hands and lips, revelling in the freedom as she alternated between rubbing her face against him and driving him nuts with her damp tongue. Before either of them knew, Jamie's shirt had found its way to the floor.

Jamie held her in his arms, so preciously, watching her face avidly, excited more and more by the whimpers emanating from her throat.

Soon, Rhea was on her knees on the floor, her face pressed to his washboard abs, her tongue flicking in and out of his navel.

"Rhea," Jamie lifted her face up to his, bending down to whisper in her ear. "I think it's my turn. Will you let me kiss you?"

"Jamie, I..." Rhea sighed. She was excited and scared at the same time. She took his hand and placed it against her breast, staring at his large hand which almost covered one whole breast. She forgot to breathe when he squeezed it gently; it felt so damn good even through the multiple layers of her clothing.

Rhea freed her arms from his hold to remove her top in a rush. Then off came her camisole. She hesitated when she saw Jamie's avid gaze on her lace-covered chest.

Jamie drew in a deep breath as he looked at the luscious twin mounds in front of him. Yes, he had seen her in a swimsuit before, but this wasn't the same. There was something about the rich cream lace of her bra which made him drool. The tips of her breasts pushed at their constriction invitingly. Jamie traced a thumb over a turgid nipple, before his eyes went to Rhea's face, always sensitive to her response. He didn't want her to run away scared.

Her eyes were shut tightly even as colour ran high on her cheeks, her dark eyelashes fluttering over them. Finally convinced she wasn't going anywhere, he bent down to take a gentle bite of the tip he had traced with his thumb, making Rhea jump.

That felt so awesome. Rhea's arms went around Jamie's neck to pull his head closer to her body. "Give me more, Jamie," she moaned.

A smile on his face, Jamie managed to remove the clasp which was holding her bra in place and threw the garment down on the floor, exposing her breasts fully before he devoured her with his gaze. "You are gorgeous," he whispered, stroking a damp tongue over an aureole.

"Jamie..." Rhea whimpered, trembling in his arms. She had never imagined it would be so wonderful to have a guy make love to her breasts. She got off the floor to sit on his lap to give him better access.

Jamie turned her away from him, her naked back pressed to his bare chest, holding her heavy breasts tenderly as they spilled over his cupped hands. He brushed his palms over the taut nipples, his face buried against her neck. "Rhea... I like you in my arms, kissing you, cuddling you, petting you. I..." He made love to her with his words, touching his lips to the sensitive spots on her neck as he gently rolled the tips of her breasts between his fingers and thumbs.

Rhea pressed against his chest, bombarded from all ends as the hair on his chest teased the sensitive skin of her back. Her pulse skittered away as she felt his tongue brush against her skin. How the hell did he know the exact points which aroused her to fever pitch?! And his hands! They played magic with her breasts. Rhea had never felt so proud of being a woman. She felt wetness pool between her thighs and rubbed her legs together restlessly, her hands holding his forearms tightly, her nails digging into them.

Jamie turned her around to the side, so that he could bend down and take a sensitive nipple into his mouth. Rhea moaned long and hard when he sucked on the sensitive tip, setting her body on fire. She clutched his head in her hands, her fingers digging into his scalp as she pulled him closer to her body, frenzied with need. She protested loudly when Jamie removed his mouth to trace a path across the valley of her chest to reach the other breast.

Jamie laughed softly, raising his eyes to look up at her, his lips still pressed to the curve of her breast.

"Don't... stop," she moaned and choked immediately when his lips closed over the tip of the other breast. "Oh yes!"

Jamie took her hand and placed it against his crotch. Rhea's eyes went wide as she rubbed her hand up and down against the bulge which she could feel through his jeans. "Jamie, I want to touch you," she pleaded.

Jamie raised his head from her breasts with reluctance and looked at her with his slumberous jade gaze. "I have a condition."

"What?" She threw her arms around his waist to press her throbbing breasts to his muscular chest. The sensitised nipples rejoiced their brush against the curly hair on his chest. "Mmm..." she bit his earlobe.

"If you touch me, there's no going back. I want to make love to you Rhea, completely." He tilted her chin to look into her eyes. "Will you let me?"

Rhea held his arm, looking at the banked fire in his green eyes. Jamie had been more than patient with her, giving her the utmost space. And it was obvious they both wanted more. The wetness between her legs and his tumescent manhood cried out for fulfilment. "Yes please," she said, burying her face in the crook of his shoulder.

With a whoop of joy, Jamie lifted Rhea in his arms and carried her to his bedroom, pushing the door open to lay her down on his bed. It took him but a few seconds to pull off his belt and jeans before he helped her remove hers. Their shoes came off next before he settled down on the bed next to her, guiding her hand to his erection, as he lay down next to her.

Rhea was fascinated as she felt him grow bigger under her caress. She sat on the bed for better access as she took him in both her hands. His arms under his head, Jamie watched her ardently as her breasts danced in front of him while she explored him thoroughly. Then he got up to push her back on the bed before kissing his way down her body, revering her with his hands and lips. Rhea almost jumped off the bed when he placed a hand against her vagina, caressing the jet-black curls which covered her femininity. He parted her legs to dip a finger in her vulva, making her moan.

Rhea felt lost. "Jamie, you're too far away. Please hold me."

He was beside her the next moment, holding her close to his body with his left arm, while his right hand continued to explore her core. He kissed her hard, before dragging his lips down to her breasts and making love to them all over again.

Rhea thrashed her legs as she felt his fingers—first one and then a second—plunge into her vagina. "Jamie... I want you."

She stared at him, disappointed when he moved away from her to open a bedside drawer, but cheered up when he removed a condom and pulled it over himself. Jamie moved above her then, parting her legs wide to draw one around his waist. "This might hurt a bit."

Rhea stared up at him for a couple of moments before saying, "I trust you," making Jamie's chest puff up with pride.

He entered her with a grunt, waiting for her to adjust to his shape and size, before pushing in. He stopped again when she yelled. "I'm sorry," he said, kissing her on her forehead, before pressing his cheek to hers, until she moved her legs again, inviting him further inside her.

And then the age-old ritual began. Jamie thrust into her, first gently and then harder, as Rhea locked both her legs around his lean waist, her head thrashing against the pillows even as her hands clutched his strong back. He kissed her, his tongue following the movement of his penis. It wasn't long before Rhea felt an orgasm rip through her body, making her moan long and loud, her nails raking down his hard back. "Jamie..." she whimpered, her eyes going wide in wonder. She watched him as he continued to pump into her, his face a study in concentration before he also groaned his release, spilling his seed into her before he fell over her supine body, totally spent.

Rhea held him close, her arms around him, pressing soft kisses wherever she could reach him. "Thank you, Jamie. That was simply wonderful," she whispered. "I've never experienced anything like it before."

Jamie buried his face into her neck, not saying anything. It had been an explosive experience for him too, shaking him to the core of his being. Though an innocent, Rhea's responses had driven him wild. And his body was already ready for an encore.

18

J amie looked at the sleeping woman in his bed as he placed the tray containing a flask with filter coffee and a jug of milk, sugar and two mugs on the side table. It was past seven and Rhea probably needed to be up. He placed a hand on her shoulder to wake her when she turned around to look up at him, her eyes open barely a slit. She looked amazingly beautiful, more than usual.

"Jamie..." Rhea opened her arms invitingly.

He bent down to kiss her hard before saying, "Good morning, sweetheart. Did you sleep well?"

"Never better," said Rhea, rubbing a hand down his bare back, startled when he winced. "What?" She got up to check for herself and was shocked to see the red marks. "Did I do that to you?" she asked him in a whisper, her eyes rounded. "I'm terribly sorry, Jamie." She tried to get out of the bed, only he wouldn't let her go.

"Don't be. You were in the throes of passion and that's surely a compliment to my prowess," he grinned.

"How can you say that, Jamie? You skin looks so red and angry. Let me get some cream to ease the pain."

"Later. Tell me something. It's past seven. Do you need to rush or do we've time for..."

"We do," grinned Rhea, even as colour rushed to her cheeks. "What's the use of being the boss if I can't go late to work?"

Jamie laughed before pulling her into his arms. "Are you recovered from last night? No pain?" he asked, concerned.

Rhea shook her head, snuggling against him. "I'm fine. And Jamie," she looked up at him, "You must tell me if I get too rough. I never would've believed it if I hadn't seen the marks on your back. I'm..."

"I'll catch the next plane home if you apologise once more," said Jamie in mock threat, stroking the sensitive skin behind her ear with his tongue. "Did I tell you how good you taste?"

"Tell me more," sighed Rhea, not interested in arguing with him.

Jamie made long and leisurely love to her, discovering more erogenous zones which made her go crazy. In turn, Rhea insisted on loving every inch of him with her hands and mouth, unable to resist biting him a few times. He showed her how it tended to arouse him rather than hurt him.

They showered together after drinking coffee, reluctant to go their separate ways. "I'm off to my work site. I'll catch you in the evening," said Jamie, watching her tug on her winter clothes, layer by layer, covering up her lovely figure.

"Can't we meet for lunch?" asked Rhea, her eyes clinging to his.

"We can. Do you wanna go out?"

"Can't we have it right here at home?" she asked, a mischievous look in her eyes.

Jamie grinned. "You're on! I'll see you at lunch then." He kissed her deeply before letting her go. "Bye."

Rhea found herself grinning at her reflection in the mirror as she brushed her hair and applied minimal make up. Life was too beautiful! All her fears of being with a man seemed to have disappeared like mist at the arrival of sunrise. Locking her front door, Rhea walked to her hotel with a spring in her step.

Ajit Parmar surreptitiously studied Rhea Bansal as she walked into the reception. He had been working with Rose Garden International as a bellhop for ten days. He had got the job through recommendation. At twenty-two, Ajit was built like a tank, tall and muscular. Claiming to be educated to middle-school level and with a smattering of spoken English to his credit, Ajit had had no trouble landing the job at the high-end hotel.

But he had another agenda altogether—to report his boss's movements to MLA Marudhanayagam. He answered directly to the politician and none else. Ajit preferred to take odd jobs which required him to wield his muscles rather than use his brains. He was an expert at breaking people's bones, though he had never killed anyone so far in his young life. He worked best with wooden clubs and knives. Luckily for him, he didn't have to carry his own knives since there were a number of those available in the hotel's multiple kitchens. Which took away the onus of coming up with an idea as to how to get past security along with his weapons.

These past ten days, Ajit had found out that as a verified employee, he had the complete run of the hotel, from the reception to the guest cottages to the restaurants to the kitchens to the shops. It perfectly suited his purpose. He had also found out his boss lived next door, alone, in a private cottage. Which particular piece of information he had already personally passed on to the MLA on the last Thursday when Ajit had his weekly off.

Ajit pushed the luggage trolley towards the back door, showing the way to the newly arrived guests. He pointed to the waiting golf cart and said to the couple, "Please sit. We take you to room." He loaded the luggage into the back of the cart. "Cottage no 58," said Ajit to Raghav, the driver, before jogging behind the cart when it took off. Ajit believed in exercise and found the constant running around kept him fitter than any gym could do. His muscles got enough work from lugging around the guests' baggage. Like now when he opened the single-bedroom cottage, before carrying the three heavy suitcases inside. He thanked the guests politely, accepting the generous tip which they gave him. Ajit didn't realise the mistake he had committed in the driver's presence.

Raghav was about to take off when he saw the guest opening his purse. He had stopped out of curiosity and was startled to see Ajit accepting a five-hundred-rupee note. It was an unwritten rule that the employees at Rose Garden International never accepted a tip. Everyone was informed about this during their induction and agreed with the management as the money charged for service on their bills was shared among all the employees in reverse proportion—the wage earners getting larger shares while the salaried employees got a nominal share. The first thing Raghav did when he got back to the main building was to walk into the reception and have a word with Shiva.

"Thank you, Raghav," said Shiva, when the driver told him about Ajit's gaffe. "Just keep the information to yourself and don't mention anything, even to Ajit."

"Sure, sir," said Raghav, nodding his greying head.

Shiva was a little disturbed at the news about Ajit. The man had been recommended by a VIP guest who dined regularly at the various restaurants in the hotel. Ajit had undergone the induction and in the hotel's history, there hadn't been a single employee who hadn't followed the rule. This wasn't good for the hotel's reputation. Normally, he would have reported this to Rhea Bansal immediately. But not this time.

There was a reason for it. Shiva had been invited to go meet Officer Vadivel at the police commissioner's office a couple of weeks ago. He had been surprised to find Jamie Scott also present at the meeting.

"Sit down, Shiva," said Vadivel, pointing to a chair. "Do you know what exactly happened that day when Inspector Kamalakannan and MLA Marudhanayagam visited Rose Garden International?" Vadivel came straight to the point.

"I think I do. Inspector Kamalakannan has been banned from visiting our hotel. What I understood is, he was trying to outsmart the hotel management by bringing the MLA along with him to ensure he was not stopped from entering the premises. Am I right?"

"Yes," Vadivel nodded, waiting for him to continue.

Shiva turned to look at the silent Australian, wondering once again what he was doing here. He continued, "And I think both of them were hoping to get a free meal, trying to take advantage of their combined powers. But Rhea ma'am took your help to remove them from the premises."

Vadivel nodded. "You're absolutely right. So, what do you think will happen now? Will the MLA take the insult lying down?"

Shiva frowned, thinking hard. "But sir, why should he get offended? The MLA could have had lunch if he was ready to pay for the meal, right? No one would have stopped him."

Vadivel grinned. "You're right, Shiva. But these rules apply to people with common decency. Marudhanayagam is a corrupt politician through and through. Have you any idea what happened to Inspector Kamalakannan after the fiasco?"

"Don't tell me he got transferred to a desert?"

Vadivel burst out laughing. "You hit the nail exactly on the head."

"What?!" Shiva's jaw dropped. He had been joking, never for a moment imagining that it must have actually happened.

Vadivel stopped laughing, his face turning serious. "Now you realise what kind of an enemy we are dealing with."

"Enemy?" Shiva scowled again. "Who's?"

"Rhea Bansal's."

Shiva turned pale. "But how, sir? Ma'am is running the hotel so well and works harder than any of us. Why should the MLA have the power to trouble her? Can't you help keep her safe from him? I mean, you being employed in the police commissioner's office and all that. Isn't that the reason why Rhea ma'am contacted you people?" He was extremely upset.

Vadivel walked around the table to lay a hand on Shiva's shoulder. "I absolutely understand where you're coming from. Let's not panic now. If I know him, the MLA will strike soon so we don't really have to wait too long. But we need to be alert. At this juncture, I feel we shouldn't worry Rhea Bansal. Which is why I decided to contact you. You are her second-in-command and have been working at the hotel from the beginning. And Jamie Scott here," he turned to look at the man, "is helping us. He's a trained fighter." Vadivel smiled at Shiva's startled face. "The advantage is, Jamie is living in Rhea's cottage as a paying guest. He can keep an eye on her. Yes, it's sheer luck he's on our side."

Shiva looked from one man to the other, a slow smile appearing on his intelligent face while his frown completely disappeared. "This is surely a stroke of luck. Now tell me what I need to do, gentlemen," he requested, sitting up straight in his chair, feeling proud to be of service to Rhea Bansal, a woman he revered.

Shiva left the police commissioner's office two hours later, totally clear about his role in the mission of saving Rhea Bansal from MLA Marudhanayagam's wrath.

Just now, Shiva took his mobile phone to send Jamie Scott a WhatsApp message.

19

Rhea stretched her arms above her head, a wide smile on her lips as she sat at her desk, staring at it, doing nothing. Which was a first for her. She couldn't remember a time in the past two decades when she hadn't been busy doing something or the other. Life had been one headlong rush from one project to the next, first at college, then at the different places of work and finally at her own business. She had even taken her holidays seriously, making a list before she left and ensuring she completed each and every sightseeing spot. Rohit had tried his best to wean her out of this habit during their recent trip to Europe while Ritvik had tried to tease her out of it, but the only thing both had managed to achieve was to have their heads bitten off.

But Jamie—Rhea's smile turned into a grin—had taught her to stop and smell the flowers, without much of an effort. He had never said anything, just *being* exactly what he was—totally patient and like a rock beside her, never once criticising her. And Rhea realised that was what had made all the difference. She was still amazed how he had landed up here in Ooty as if Destiny had sent him down especially for her. He never seemed to look outside for either occupation or entertainment. He had found his own interior designing project while also doing all the sightseeing he wanted. He took himself around Ooty by cycle, motorbike or on horseback. He definitely was one of a kind and had all her admiration.

And look at the way he dealt with her. He never pushed, had never given her the impression he wanted more from Rhea than what she was ready to give. He had been there, patiently in the background, all the while.

In fact, it was Rhea who had used him, every time. She had honed her lovemaking skills on him. Rhea blushed when she thought about it. She had initiated the kisses. It wasn't as if he hadn't wanted to kiss her. But she had the freedom to kiss or not to. He had left it all on her, taking a step forward only if she was ready. His patience had paid off; the fire had built, slowly, but steadily.

Rhea turned redder, if such a thing was even possible. Till the time he had laid out that small condition. If she wanted to touch him, he would make love to her completely. And how desperate she had been to touch him! She had felt his erection many times when they had necked, but had chosen to ignore it, out of fear more than anything else. Finally, curiosity had driven her, that and the fire in her womb, the call for physical completion.

Had it been worth it?

Oh yes! Way more than worth it. Rhea stood at the window, grinning like an idiot as a squirrel squeaked on its way up a tree limb. She felt all woman, replete with satisfaction. Jamie had finally *shown* her it was truly worth it to let go of her control. She still continued to feel safe, though only in his arms.

Had she fallen in love?

Rhea wasn't sure. But just now, it didn't seem to matter. She was happy and maybe, just maybe, finally at peace.

The smile refused to leave Rhea's face the whole day.

20

Jamie was at Somasekhar's new home when his phone pinged. Seeing Shiva's name, he checked the message. "Unusual behaviour by newly hired bellhop. Can we meet?"

He responded saying, "Sure, if post lunch will work for you."

Jamie received a confirmation almost immediately from Rhea's manager. Removing the frown from his face, he continued to supervise the work until noon and left immediately after, refusing the lunch the lady of the house offered. He couldn't wait to get back to Rhea, still incredulous about the memory of the previous night he had spent in her arms.

Jamie kickstarted his hired motorbike and roared away towards Rhea's cottage. He had taken the precaution of entering and leaving her home from the back gate which was half a kilometre away from the hotel's main entrance. He had even stopped using the swimming pool nowadays. Jamie didn't want the MLA's mole to find out that she didn't live alone in her house.

Rhea reached barely a few minutes after Jamie let himself into her home. She threw her arms around his neck and kissed him on his mouth. "Whoa!" said Jamie, grinning widely before lifting her in his arms to swing her around.

"Jamie..." She clung to his shoulders, laughing. "Put me down."

He stopped swinging but still held her aloft, rubbing his face against her soft breasts.

"Hey!" Rhea's voice was choked as she felt the swift rise of desire clogging her throat. She held his head close against her body, saying, "I'm going to have you for lunch."

Jamie laughed as he carried her off to his bedroom.

Almost an hour later, Rhea peeped up into his face to say softly, "I'm famished. Let's order lunch."

Jamie looked at her in mock horror, a hand against his heart. "What?! After that sumptuous lunch? No way!"

"Idiot!" Rhea threw a pillow at him, laughing as she pulled on his full-sleeved t-shirt over her head, rolling the sleeves many times over. "So, what do you want to have?"

"I have a stock of pizzas in the freezer. Shall I warm those? Unless you want to order something else?"

"You mean you made the pizzas?" Rhea asked him curiously.

"Yeah," he said, pulling on his boxers.

"Perfect. Let's go get them."

He threw an arm around her shoulders as they walked side by side to the kitchen. Jamie poured Rhea a glass of wine while he removed two large pizzas with different toppings—pepperoni and chicken along with onions, tomato, corn and broccoli, topped with mozzarella cheese—and placed them in the microwave. A wonderful aroma wafted from the oven, making Rhea's stomach growl.

Jamie set the table with plates and cutlery before he brought the pizzas over and sliced them. He watched in fascination as Rhea bit into a corner of the chicken pizza before exclaiming, "Hmm... yummy! Do tell me if you need a job as chef any time," she said, grinning at him cheekily.

Jamie laughed. "Maybe, thanks." He didn't tell her he planned to be her house-husband if she would accept him.

Jamie dressed up to leave immediately after lunch, much to Rhea's disappointment. "Sorry to leave in a hurry, sweetheart," he said, pressing a brief kiss on her lips. "But I've got an appointment at 2.30. I'll catch you in the evening."

He left through the back door and gate, riding on his bike to meet Shiva at his home. The latter had taken permission to leave for an hour citing he had some urgent personal work.

"Please come in, Mr Scott," Shiva invited Jamie into his home. "Would you like to have some tea?"

"Nothing for me, mate. And do call me Jamie," Jamie insisted, sitting down on the living room sofa. "Fill me in on what happened."

Shiva told him briefly about what he had heard from Raghav. "As I told you last week, we have three new people who joined us after the MLA's visit. Elango and Geetha came through an employment agency. Elango helps handle the stocks and provisions, while Geetha has joined the accounts team. Ajit Parmar was given a job because he came highly recommended by a regular client of ours. And since it's a bellhop's job, he doesn't really need special qualifications. I've been keeping an eye on all three of them, until I found Ajit's behaviour a bit odd today." Shiva handed Jamie a pen drive which had the CCTV footage of Ajit's movements from the day he had joined. "This will help you find out more about the man. In the meanwhile, I'll keep an eye out on the other two people also."

"Perfect, Shiva. Can you message me Ajit Parmar's address, cell number and his shift timings, including his day off?"

"I have the details right here," said Shiva, handing him a printed sheet of paper.

Jamie ran his eyes over the sheet and smiled at Shiva, saying, "Excellent, mate! Thanks a ton!"

"Not at all, sir, as long as Rhea ma'am comes to no harm." His voice shook with emotion.

"She won't, I promise," said Jamie reassuringly, a deadly expression in his eyes. "You keep me posted regarding the activities at the hotel. I'm avoiding being seen there as much as possible, if you realise."

Shiva nodded before saying, "Rose Garden will be hosting the yearly Winter Fair over the weekend of December 10th & 11th. We'll have large crowds of people holding stalls as well as visiting the fair. While we do our best to keep security tight, we can't have enough people watching such a big, rollicking crowd which has the complete run of the hotel." He looked worried.

Jamie nodded. "Thanks again, mate. I'll be in touch. See you!" He shook Shiva's hand before going directly to Vadivel's office to have a word with him.

A man following Ajit Parmar on his next day off brought back the news of the latter's visit to the MLA's office.

"Shiva's guess was right, Jamie. Ajit Parmar is our man," said Vadivel, confirming the news to Jamie on Thursday evening.

21

Jamie looked curiously at the gnarled old man who entered Somasekhar's new home. He walked with a bit of a slouch, though his eyesight seemed sharp when he looked up at the foreigner.

Somasekhar came forward to introduce the two of them. "Jamie, I'd like you to meet my neighbour, Kandasamy Uncle. He's ninety-two plus. Uncle, this is Jamie Scott. He's designing the interior for our home."

Kandasamy shook Jamie's hand in an absent-minded fashion, staring at the younger man's face, his mouth wide. "Scott," he said, a frown of concentration on his face. "Would you by any chance be related to a man called Jason Scott?" he asked.

While Jamie looked at the old man in wonder, Somasekhar shushed his neighbour. "Uncle, Jamie is from a foreign country. You are confused I think..."

Jamie raised a hand to stop him, continuing to look at Kandasamy. "Sir, did you know Jason Scott? You are probably talking about my grandfather."

Kandasamy gave him a toothless grin, raising a hand to pat Jamie on his arm. "I just knew it. You look exactly like how Jason Sir used to look, all those years back. I worked as their groom in those days. I..." He thought hard before saying, "I'm not sure about the year, but it was during the British Raj. Jason Sir and Barbara Madam took such wonderful care of me and my family during their stay here." Kandasamy's voice wobbled with emotion as he recalled the olden times.

Jamie went forward and hugged the old man, feeling emotional himself. He made Kandasamy sit down, going on his knees on the floor next to him, so they could see eye-to-eye comfortably. "I've never seen my grandfather. He died many years before I was born. But my grandma—Barbara—spoke to me a lot about Ooty. Which is the reason I came over for a holiday here. But this is simply amazing. I never thought I'd get to meet someone who used to know them so well."

Somasekhar looked from one man to the other as they chatted, forgetting to shut his dropping jaw.

Kandasamy rested his balding head on Jamie's strong shoulder, wiping his eyes. "I was so happy when I got a job with them. They were such kind employers. I'm able to speak in English to you today because of Barbara Madam. She used to teach me every day, after I finished my work at the stables. They had eight horses. There was this big carriage drawn by four matching horses, all jet black in colour with white stars on their foreheads and white tails. Then there were the two brown mares which were used to draw a small high perch phaeton. The other two horses were used for riding by sir and madam. Their home was so lovely and such a happy place. There was a big celebration when their baby was born. Let me see, would that be your father? His name was Nathan."

Jamie grinned widely at the old man, nodding his head vigorously. "Yes, that's my father."

"Aah, and I remember they had booked a pony for the little boy. Where is Master Nathan now?"

"He lives in Australia."

"Oh yes! That's where they went, taking the small boy. Barbara Madam cried for many days before they left. She didn't want to go. I know Jason Sir was not happy either." Kandasamy sighed heavily. "But what to do? It's all fate."

He fell silent for some time, obviously reliving those days of glory, before suddenly turning and telling Jamie, "You know, they gifted me with an acre of farming land before they left, along with my favourite horse, so that I didn't have to find another job to maintain my family." Kandasamy's voice shook with emotion. "Call it luck or fate, I grew as a farmer and own five acres of land now with many eucalyptus trees in it. I even have a proper brick house in place of the hut which I used to live in." He wiped his eyes once again, smiling at the strapping young man. It could have been his employer of old—Jason Scott—who was smiling back at him now. The same bright green eyes, golden hair which was darker at the roots, sharp nose and strong chin—the man in front of him looked exactly like his grandfather.

They chatted some more as Kandasamy reminisced over those grand old days. There wasn't a thing the man didn't know about horses. Jamie kept listening to him, not saying much, fascinated to hear first-hand about his grandparents' life in Ooty, the hill-station which had been their home before they moved to Australia. Jamie was sure his father would be equally interested in knowing more about Jason and Barbara's brief tenure in India.

"Can you recall the location of their home, sir? It was called Rose Garden in those days. I have been searching for it on and off, but I have no clue to the address. And I am sure Ooty must have changed a lot since 1947."

Kandasamy nodded sagely. "Of course, I remember. And you shouldn't call me sir. I used to be a servant in your grandparents' home," he smiled.

Jamie shook his head. "With due respect to your age, my grandparents wouldn't expect any less from me. Please allow me to address you as sir."

"Call me uncle then. That's what they all do," he said, pointing to the silent Somasekhar. "And yes, your grandfather built a two-storey mansion—rather small by British standards they said—over a large piece of land, must be around fifteen acres if I remember right. There was also a smaller cottage built a little further away. I think they planned that one for retirement or something like that, I am not sure. There was a clock tower in the centre. But then, all mansions built by the British have clock towers," Kandasamy laughed. "Do you know the Emerald Lake? It is to the north of Ooty."

Jamie nodded, wondering how close his grandparents' old property must have been to Rhea's hotel.

"Rose Garden was very close to it. They sold the house and land to someone only a few weeks before leaving. I don't know the person's name, but I am sure we can get the information from the Ooty municipal records," said the old man.

Jamie nodded again, not really interested in finding the owner. All he wanted to see was the house, if it still existed in its original form. "Thank you, uncle. I'll look out for it. You say it was to the north of the lake, right?"

"No, no." Kandasamy shook his head. "The Emerald Lake is to the north of Ooty. The house was to the east, about four km from where the bazaar is these days. Have you visited the market?"

"Yes, many times," said Jamie, a small frown of concentration on his face. He had cycled many times to the bazaar to purchase groceries. Kandasamy obviously didn't have an address. For all they knew, the postal address also may have changed. He wondered if he could persuade the old man to go with him to check the area out. Well, probably on another day. Jamie planned to scout the area around the lake by himself first. "Let me check out all the properties in the area. There aren't all that many, I think."

Somasekhar spoke for the first time in a long time. "You are right. There aren't too many properties there. There's Rose Garden International, another resort further down and the market on this side. Other than these, there are only gardens and tea plantations all around the area. People flock there to see the many fishes and birds which throng in and around the lake. I can't recall many other buildings in the area."

Jamie shrugged. "Let me see."

The next day, Jamie went by horse and checked all properties within a radius of five km on either side of Rose Garden International, but was disappointed not to find any which could have belonged to his grandparents. He wondered if Kandasamy would agree to go with him on a visit. Jamie decided to ask him.

22

Over the next few days, however, Jamie didn't have time to think of his grandparents' home as Vadivel had confirmed it was Ajit Parmar who was the MLA's mole. He took to visiting Somasekhar's home for half an hour in the morning and another fifteen minutes in the late afternoon, spending the rest of his time close to the area where he knew Rhea was present. It wasn't easy as he had to be careful not to reveal his presence. He was in constant touch with Shiva. Waiting for the enemy to strike was the most difficult task for anyone. It was a good thing Shiva had told him about the upcoming Winter Fair at Rose Garden International as the hotel began its preparations for the grand event.

Jamie wondered how he could be a part of the event, without simply being a visitor. He needed a valid excuse to be present on the premises from morning till night without revealing his connection to Rhea.

"What's this Winter Fair which I'm hearing so much about?" Jamie asked Rhea that night. She was lying naked in his arms, a finger lazily tracing patterns on his bare chest.

Rhea looked up at him and smiled. "Oh, you heard about that! It's a gala we set up on a yearly basis. Artists, sculptors, curio traders, chocolatiers, perfumed oil traders and many others from all over Ooty set up their stalls at the fair. Other food stalls are put up by Rose Garden's five restaurants and delicatessen. We charge outside tradesmen for the space while they also give us a percentage of their profits. All these monies and the total profits from the food stalls are donated to an NGO dedicated to aid poor kids in gaining Life Skills Empowerment. It's usually held over the second weekend of December and has been a terrific success all these years."

Jamie bent forward to kiss Rhea on her forehead, his admiration for her going up by a few more notches. "I don't suppose I need to ask whose idea it is," he said.

Rhea shrugged, drawing his eyes to her breast as it bounced against his chest. "Well, the lady who runs the NGO went to college with me and I know Priya's absolutely passionate about her cause."

"Hmm..." Jamie swirled his tongue around the tip of her breast before taking it into his mouth, suckling gently.

Rhea tangled her fingers into his hair, pulling his head closer to her body, heat pooling between her legs, as they both lost the thread of their conversation.

It was a long time before Jamie said, "I'd love to be a part of this venture."

Rhea looked up curiously at his handsome face. "What stall do you plan to set up?"

"Pencil sketches of people. I also have a few watercolours which I've painted of the local flora and fauna. I will be holding a sale of those too."

"What?! You draw and paint?" Rhea looked up at him in wide-eyed surprise.

"Guilty," said Jamie, a smile on his face.

"This I must see. When did you plan to show me?" she glared at him accusingly, getting off the bed to stand with her arms akimbo.

Jamie looked up at the proud and naked woman who stood in front of him—falling in love with her more and more—and laughed. He went to a table drawer to remove the fourteen watercolours which he had made on 16x20 canvases before he gestured for Rhea to go closer.

He placed the paintings on the table, throwing an arm around her waist, before showing them to her one by one. The paintings were brilliant in their simplicity. There was one of a wood-pecker with a white belly, another of a squirrel holding a nut in its forepaws halfway up a tree branch, and a third of a rose bush with a cluster of half-open blush pink buds. There was even one of Gulliver and another of Sovereign, set against the background of the hotel. Rhea didn't know much about art, but even she could see that the artworks in front of her were exceptionally good. There were no empty spaces on the canvases as they were all fully coloured—either with the blue sky in the background or the lake, tree or grass—with one centre point of attraction. The last two paintings were the best of the lot. The first was of a pink sun rising behind the dazzling green of the hills while the other showed an orange sun sliding into the calm and beautiful blue-green lake, just before twilight.

"Jamie, you made all these during your stay in Ooty?! They look so beautiful." Rhea's voice was reverent.

Jamie pressed his cheek to her hair. "Thanks. These are my best works till date." He wasn't going to tell her that his creativity had transcended to a different level after meeting her, the love of his life.

"I love them. Will you let me buy some of these?"

"I thought of selling them at the Winter Fair to raise money for the NGO, along with the pencil sketches of the visitors. I can make more for you later, if you're okay with it."

Rhea nodded her head vigorously before kissing his shoulder. "Perfect. These are bound to sell like hot cakes. Do you plan to have them framed?"

"What do you suggest?"

"I say it would be a great idea," she grinned. She threw her arms around his neck, pulling his head down. "Jamie, do you think I'm falling in love with you?" she whispered against his ear. "I'm scared of the word actually. It has brought me nothing but disappointment."

"Don't use the word then," Jamie smiled, a hand under her chin as he lifted her face up to his. "I'm here for you, for as long as you want me—as your friend, and as your lover. So who needs a label for what you feel for me?"

"Jamie..." Rhea kissed him, overcome by emotion. "You are the best."

He kissed her right back before drawing her attention to a notebook. "What's this?" she asked, curious.

"Open it and see for yourself," he invited.

Rhea opened the first page and her mouth fell open as she stared spellbound at her own face as it laughed back at her. It was only a pencil sketch, but it brought her to life on the paper. She sagged back against his firm body, opening the next page with a trembling hand. Her own face glared back at her, her black eyes glowing furiously. She could have been looking into a mirror which threw up black and white images. The more she turned the pages, the more she saw of herself—a soft and gentle expression as she stroked Gulliver's forehead, her face polite when she dealt with a client. There was one where she had such an expression of adoration that Rhea was sure she must have been eyeing Jamie. She turned around to look at him, "Do I look like this when I see you?"

Jamie nodded. "You've got the exact same expression on your face right now."

"Thank you, Jamie." She so hoped he was also falling for her. Why would he draw so many sketches of her otherwise? Lovingly too, or that is how they appeared to her. The notebook was full, every page having Rhea's face stamped across it.

Jamie held her close, his arms around her waist. "You inspire me."

J amie met Vadivel once again and spoke to him about the Winter Fair. Both the men were in agreement that if Marudhanayagam meant to strike, the fair would probably be the best time. They actually looked forward to it so the tension would end once and for all.

"I've fixed up with Rhea to hold a sketching stall at the fair. I'm going to push for the prime position so as to keep an eye on everyone who steps in," said Jamie.

"We shouldn't forget that Ajit Parmar is already ensconced on the premises. Shiva might be too busy with other activities to keep an eye on him. I'm thinking of bringing over a few of my men in civil clothes and stationing them inside the hotel on both days. The best thing would be to tell Rhea Bansal that we are doing it as a measure of precaution. I only hope she doesn't refute the idea," sighed Vadivel.

"You should sell the idea to her saying it's more for the safety of the public than anything else. If she thinks it's for her security, she's never going to agree. It's best if you cook up some story actually, about having received information of a terror threat or whatever, something which can't be announced publicly," said Jamie, a mischievous smile on his face.

"Are you considering a career in story-writing?" asked Vadivel, laughing at the other man. "I suppose it's an idea. I'll get my boss to convince the lady."

"Which might be a good idea," agreed Jamie. "She's surely a tough nut to crack."

Vadivel grinned at his new friend. "You've come to know her really well in the short time you've been in Ooty," he teased.

Jamie laughed. "Not as much as I'd like to, believe me, my friend."

Vadivel nodded. "There are ten days to go for the fair. I'll get Commissioner Sakthivel to talk to Rhea Bansal on the Thursday before the event. What say?"

"Perfect." Jamie stood up to leave. "I'll be seeing you then. Don't forget that the MLA knows your face."

"No way are you going to keep me out of the fair, Jamie! I'll be there, even if I need to disguise myself. But I'm sure it won't come to that. A little bit of police security is the accepted norm at such galas. That shouldn't make the MLA suspect anything."

"I suppose," said Jamie, unable to stop the sudden sigh which broke out. "I can't say that I'm not worried, mate," he admitted.

Vadivel patted the other man on his shoulder. "Don't worry. Rats aren't all that difficult to corner."

"True." Shrugging off the sudden feeling of morbidity, Jamie left to go to Somasekhar's new home.

Somasekhar's house would need another three days to be completely ready. The three younger ones in the family were too thrilled while Somasekhar and Padmaja were appreciative. "Our house is turning out so beautifully," said Sathya, shaking Jamie's hand in greeting. "We're so lucky you turned up in Ooty at a perfect time for a holiday."

Jamie laughed, feeling pleased. "I suppose it works both ways. It's lucky I found a project waiting for me just when I decided to extend my visit. Oh, by the way, I would like to visit Kandasamy Uncle. Could you give me the directions to his home?"

"Sure," said Somasekhar, stepping out of his new house and pointing out the direction. "You probably will need to ride about five minutes on your motorbike to the left. You will find a square cottage, painted in a bright blue, behind wooden gates, with a lot of creepers running over the wall. That's his home."

"Thank you. I will see you tomorrow," said Jamie, firing his bike.

Kandasamy was sitting on his balcony, wrapped up in a thick shawl. "Welcome, welcome," he called out cheerfully when he saw Jamie.

Jamie parked his bike and walked up to the old man to shake his hand. "Good afternoon, Uncle. How have you been?"

"Just fine." He turned towards the entrance to his home and shouted, "Ponnamma, *rendu chaaya kondukittu vaa*." Then turning to his guest, he continued, "Tell me, did you find Rose Garden?"

"That's what I came to talk to you about. I couldn't find it. Will you be able to go with me to show the place? Only if it's not too much trouble, that is."

Kandasamy shook his head vigorously. "What trouble? Of course, I will go with you. Just wait. My daughter is getting tea for both of us. Let's first drink that before leaving."

"Now? But... Uncle, I only have my motorbike with me. Let me get a car, maybe tomorrow. You..."

"What? You think this old man can't ride a bike?" Kandasamy laughed, gesturing to Ponnamma to come forward and place the steel tumblers with tea on a small table. "I've lived most of my life on the backs of horses. I go riding every day till this day. What's a motorbike ride to me? Go on, drink the tea before it gets cold."

Jamie smiled, lifting a tumbler and sipping the fragrant tea. "Then will you go with me now?"

Kandasamy nodded again, gulping down the hot beverage as Jamie watched him in surprise. "Yes, I'll go with you." He waited for the younger man to finish his tea before getting up. "Let's go."

Jamie was only too happy to take Kandasamy with him as they went scouting for Rose Garden. As they passed through the market, the old man commented, "This same place was a market then too. Only it used to look so different. Not very far now. We should get there in another fifteen minutes, if there's no traffic. Keep going straight."

Jamie was a bit surprised. They were directly on their way to Rhea's hotel which was about fifteen minutes away. What other property was Kandasamy talking about?

Just as Jamie was about to cross the gates of Rose Garden International, Kandasamy exclaimed,

"Stop, stop! This is the place. I suppose somebody has converted it into a hotel," he said, looking at the freshly painted structure. "I have so been out of touch, what with being housebound with bronchitis over the past few years. I suppose this hotel is new. I wasn't aware and that's why I couldn't tell you about it." He slapped his forehead lightly before continuing, "Do you see that?" he pointed up at the clock tower, "That was what I was telling you about. Your grandfather, Jason sir, had imported the clock all the way from London and had it fitted there. Doesn't it look grand? I wonder if the hotel owner will allow us to see the place? And do you notice the other building on the left, beyond the fence?" He pointed to what was now Rhea's home, "That's the smaller cottage I spoke to you about."

Jamie simply stood there; his eyes open wide in surprise. He had been staying on this very property from the day he had arrived in Ooty. And now it looked like this had belonged to his grandparents once upon a time. This was simply too amazing for words.

"Are you sure this is the place, Uncle?" Even as he asked the question, Jamie already knew the answer. Despite his age, Kandasamy's faculties were in perfect condition and the man had been living here all his life.

Kandasamy laughed. "Of course, I am. You can always check the municipal records in case you want to. But I know the place like the back of my own hand. Those days, there were just the two buildings. The rest of the area was empty land, with a few trees and very many rose bushes. Oh, you see the board there? They have even named the hotel Rose Garden International, not bothering to change the name your grandmother gave her house. That's so nice of them."

Jamie was excited. Would Rhea know what the place had been called originally? He would have to find out. Just as he was on the verge of guiding Kandasamy into the hotel, he recalled Ajit Parmar's presence. No, this was not the right time to let it be known that he was close to Rhea. With a sigh of disappointment, Jamie decided to talk to her about it later that night.

The two of them stood there admiring the hotel even as Kandasamy reminisced over some more incidents from the Scotts' lives seven decades ago before Jamie took him back to his house. Then he remembered the paintings which he carried in a folder, lying in the storage compartment of the bike and decided to go in search of the frame-maker Sathya had highly recommended. He selected suitable frames for the paintings, paid an advance and instructed the man to deliver the completed lot directly to Rose Garden International, in charge of Shiva, the manager. Jamie didn't want anyone seeing him carry the paintings from Rhea's cottage to the hotel.

All this, Jamie kept doing mechanically, his mind still thunderstruck from what he had discovered about his grandparents' home.

24

Rhea looked at Jamie as he paced the length of the living room, a surprised look on her face. She hadn't known him long, but she would never have believed the Jamie she knew could get so restless.

Half a day was gone since Kandasamy had told Jamie that Rose Garden International was set on the same property which his grandparents used to own. While the old man had sounded so convincing, Jamie had been thinking and thinking some more even as his excitement slowly fizzled out. What if Kandasamy was confused? Suddenly, Jamie was a bit scared of finding out the truth. If he didn't ask Rhea, he would never know. What did it matter? If he asked her and she told him it wasn't the original cottage, Jamie was bound to feel disappointed. Wouldn't it be better not to ask at all?

Which is why he was restless, burning the living room carpet.

Rhea took a sip from her cup of green tea, her eyes moving back and forth, not saying anything as she didn't want to disturb him. Jamie looked adorable, hot actually, in a pair of cotton shorts and a sleeveless vest. She smiled as she studied his bold features, so glad she could do it openly, unlike the time when he was just a guest at her hotel.

"What?" Jamie stopped in front of her, leaning down to place his hands on the arms of her sofa, an eyebrow up in query. "What's so funny?"

"Funny? Nothing is funny," she said, grinning at him.

Jamie couldn't stop an answering smile from breaking out on his face as he looked at her gorgeous features. "In that case, what's making you grin from one ear to the other?"

"Oh that!" Rhea laughed. "I'm simply feeling happy; excited actually, that you're my lover."

Jamie pulled her out of the sofa, removing the cup from her hand, and wrapped his arms around her, his hand brushing the back of a thigh. "Rhea."

"Something's bothering you," said Rhea, pressing her lips to his rough cheek. "Do you want to talk about it?"

Jamie sighed, surprising Rhea more than ever. He ran a restless hand over the back of his head, looking deeply into her eyes. "I should, I think. But... I don't know."

Rhea hugged him close. "Why don't you get it off your chest?"

Jamie let go of her before walking away to sit down on the other sofa. Taking a deep breath, he said, "I... do you remember I told you my grandparents used to live in Ooty some seventy years ago?"

Rhea nodded, sitting down on an adjacent sofa. "Yeah, you told me that. They moved to Australia since the British were all leaving India."

"Yeah. I was curious about the place they used to live in. Coincidentally, it used to be called Rose Garden." Jamie rubbed his hands over his face before continuing, "When I was checking for hotels in Ooty, I chose yours because of the similarity in the names, actually." He looked sheepish now.

"Wait a minute! The main building which houses the reception," she looked at him enquiringly, continuing when he nodded, "It's the original building which was on this land, along with this cottage right here where we are sitting. And yes," a light of excitement came into her eyes, "It was called Rose Garden. I felt the name was perfect and decided to keep it. Are you saying your grandparents used to live right here?" Her voice was a whisper now.

Jamie jumped off his sofa to wander around aimlessly, before turning in her direction. "Don't you think it's too much of a coincidence? How do we know for sure?" He told her about Kandasamy and the old groom's conviction that this was the property. "But," Jamie swallowed, "I... don't know. I'm unable to absorb the magnitude of it, I suppose."

"Wait a minute. I think I can help you find proof. The people I bought the property from were NRIs. They were the second owners as their father had bought it from the original owners who had built it. The documents have the exact dates on them. Unfortunately, we can't access them immediately as I've placed them in my bank locker. But there's something else. The NRI family never lived in this place and kept it locked up all those years. When I purchased the property, I came across two trunks which had a lot of old stuff like clothes, diaries and a few photographs." Rhea jumped up suddenly, snapping her fingers. "Jamie, those trunks must have belonged to your people. You know what?" She walked up to him and held his arm tightly, totally excited, "The first time I saw you I thought you looked familiar. I had planned to check you out on the net, but didn't bother after we got to know each other and forgot all about it. Now I know why." She paused for effect.

"What?" Jamie's heartbeat quickened. "Why did you think I seemed familiar?"

"There were some photographs in one of those trunks. The man in them looked exactly like you."

Jamie grinned weakly. "You mean I look like that man. Rhea, tell me you didn't throw away those trunks," he pleaded, his green eyes shining with eagerness.

Rhea shook her head, grinning widely at him. "Nope. I have kept them safe in my attic. How could I throw away so much of rich history? I thought what in case someone came back for them? And Jamie, that's exactly what you've done." She was completely unaware of the love brimming in her charcoal gaze, startling the man in front of her.

"Show me," said Jamie as Rhea took his hand to lead him to the bedroom opposite his and pointed to the attic there which was closed with wooden shutters.

"That's where those trunks are. I'm pretty sure they belonged to your grandparents."

An hour later, Jamie sat on the floor of the room, sifting lovingly through the contents of the trunks, a soft smile on his face. Rhea had left him alone, appreciating that he might want some privacy as he connected with his ancestors. There were three photos in all, all studio portraits, though faded and a bit brown around the edges. The first one was of his father as a baby, the second one was of his grandparents and the third, with all three of them together.

And then there was his grandmother's missing diary from 1945!

It was three more hours later when Jamie walked into Rhea's bedroom and lay down next to her, burying his face against her breasts. He wasn't really surprised when her arms went around his shoulders, gathering him close, her hand moving soothingly down his back. They went to sleep, holding each other.

25

The next morning, Jamie went to the front of the hotel, staring at it with a whole new perspective. Would his grandmother have stood at this very same point looking at the clock tower from this particular angle? He walked further away towards the gate to see the building from there and was startled to see a glow surrounding not just the building but the whole of the area, covering all the cottages too. The soft light shimmered in the sunlight, like a protective bubble enclosing Rose Garden International.

The sentence in Barbara's diary came to Jamie's mind: *I see a glow surrounding our home whenever I look at it in the morning sunlight.* And she had also mentioned Jason had poured his love into every single brick which went into building their home. From where he was standing, Jamie could actually believe his grandmother's words.

There was a smile on his face when Jamie walked into the reception. He gave an imperceptible nod to Shiva, having noted that Ajit Parmar was on duty as the man was busy sifting through some luggage which belonged to the guests who were checking out that morning.

Turning left, Jamie went into the wing which used to house the kitchen and dining area in yonder days. Now, the whole area was used for stocking provisions, with three walk-in freezers to store dairy, meat and fruits and vegetables.

The other wing, which used to house the library, had been turned into three separate rooms which held the stock of bed-sheets, towels, bedding and other necessary items required for the guest cottages.

Jamie concluded the bedrooms must have been on the first floor. Suddenly realising he had never been upstairs, he walked up a wooden, carpeted staircase on the right and reached the top level. The ceiling had wooden beams running across them with a pointed roof in the centre. The bedrooms didn't exist anymore. They had been knocked together to form a large room which was the hotel's bar and discotheque—High and Magic! Jamie smiled. Rhea had been consistent with the rose theme. His grandmother would have been so happy.

Jamie realised from deep within that Ooty was the place he was going to settle in. His roots were here. And Rhea was the woman he wanted to spend the rest of his life with. He took the stairs two at a time and went directly to the reception.

"Hi, I'm hoping to book a stall for the upcoming Winter Fair," he told Shiva.

"Sure sir. Will that be for one day or two?"

Half an hour later, after filling out a form and paying the fee amount, Jamie Scott got a valid excuse for being present at Rose Garden International on both days of the Winter Fair, from morning till night.

26

Marudhanayagam looked at his reflection in the mirror, turning first to the left and then to the right. Originally, he had baulked at the idea of wearing a three-piece suit. Despite the cold weather in Ooty, the MLA preferred to wear a pristine white dhoti and a white linen full-shirt. It had become a kind of uniform for him. After all, he rarely stepped into the open, moving from his centrally heated home to his centrally heated office via a car equipped with heater.

But Ajit Parmar had advised him strongly to make sure he looked different. The MLA in a suit and hat will be almost unrecognisable. Thinking long and hard, the politician couldn't help but like the idea. Now, looking at himself in the mirror, he truly appreciated the advice given by his henchman. He wondered if even his wife would recognise him now. He turned when the lady walked into the room.

For a moment, Sankari was thrown, wondering who the stranger was, who had dared to walk into her bedroom. Her eyes went wide even as her jaw dropped—in slow motion—when she met her husband's eyes in the mirror.

"Is that you, *Mama*?"

Marudhanayagam turned around with a smile. "What do you think?"

"You look so handsome." Sankari felt extremely proud as she stared at her husband in wonder.

"You mean I didn't before?" he asked her, a twinkle in his eyes.

Sankari turned red, spluttering. "Of course not. I mean... you always look handsome, *Mama*. But..."

Marudhanayagam laughed. His wife was an innocent and was completely ignorant of what the politician got up to in the name of entertainment. She was totally unaware of the instances when he cheated on his marriage vows and those were aplenty. He had no qualms about forcing himself on women either. But in his marriage, he was a gentle husband, undemanding. Well, there was a reason for that. Sankari's father held the purse-strings. Velusamy Nadar turned a blind eye to his son-in-law's straying. *Men will be men* was the old man's favourite dialogue. Velusamy had laid just the one condition to his son-in-law: his daughter should be happy at all times, at all costs.

"Are you going somewhere?" Sankari looked unhappy. "I thought you might spend the day with me as it is Saturday."

Marudhanayagam looked at her, aghast. He hadn't expected this. "I... er... I thought I will..."

"You know the 5-star hotel you had been talking so much about? Rose Garden International? You said we could go there and spend a whole day. Can we go today? I believe they are hosting a fair. Many of my friends are going there with their families."

The couple had no children, despite Sankari and her parents visiting every temple in Tamil Nadu during their marriage of twelve years. Just now, Marudhanayagam thought quickly on his feet. If her friends and their families were going to be present there, the chances were dim of him getting his work done—that of taking revenge on Rhea Bansal. He could do without familiar faces in the vicinity. It would make better sense to go there today with his wife in tow, keep her happy and go again the next day—alone. "Why not? Sometimes *na* Sankari, you do come up with such brilliant ideas. Get ready then and we'll leave in half an hour. Is that okay with you?"

Sankari was thrilled as she nodded her head vigorously, a wide grin on her face. "Oh yes!"

Marudhanayagam pulled his hat low down on his forehead as he and Sankari stepped down from their car close to the hotel reception. Driver Dhana rushed out to purchase two of the expensive tickets and handed them reverently to his boss. "We will be here till late evening, Dhana. You have your lunch and wait for us," instructed Marudhanayagam, before walking away with his wife. He did his best to keep his staff happy since he knew that it helped in the long run.

Sankari stared wide-eyed at the gala atmosphere with a large crowd of people dressed in their winter best. There were colourful hot air balloons floating up in the sky, a number of them advertising a variety of ware available in the stalls. Air-conditioned tents had been set up along the length of the property to the left, taking one through the building housing the hotel's shops. She stopped at the first stall, her mouth agape as she stared at the picture of a Chestnut headed bee-eater sitting on a tree branch; her hand clutching her husband's. Sankari didn't know the bird's name but recognised it from having seen a number of them around on the trees in their compound. The artist had caught the details to perfection in the picture. "Can we buy that?"

Marudhanayagam stopped to look at the picture which his wife was pointing at, eyeing the price tag at the corner. Rs. 10,000—an exorbitant amount for such a small painting. He personally couldn't see what the excitement was about. But then, it was her father's money they will be spending. He turned this way and that to see who was running the stall when his eyes fell on the foreigner with golden hair. The man was at an easel, drawing something with a pencil in his hand while a small child sat on a stool in front of him. The MLA drew his wife's attention to the man.

Sankari walked behind the foreigner to see what he was drawing and her mouth opened in a surprised O when she saw the speed at which his pencil moved on the canvas as the child's face came alive on the sheet.

"Do you want him to draw your face?" asked her husband indulgently.

She nodded her head. "Yes, please. And *Mama*, can we have your picture also made?"

Marudhanayagam laughed. He was in a great mood as he felt much closer to his target. "Why not?" he shrugged.

Sankari waited for the artist to complete the child's drawing before approaching him. "Can you draw my husband's face?" she asked politely.

"And my wife's too," said Marudhanayagam, removing his hat to finger comb his hair away from his narrow forehead.

Jamie's expression showed no recognition when he realised he was facing the evil politician himself, the moment the other man removed his hat. He had only seen pictures of the man wearing a kind of local costume in white. He had never thought the man might turn up in a natty suit. It was a good thing he had stopped to speak and that too after removing his hat. Jamie wondered if he had meant to be disguised and immediately realised that's exactly what the man had done. "Sure," said Jamie now. "I can do two separate pictures or one of both of you, if you prefer it that way."

"Really!" Sankari clapped her hands with joy. "That would be so nice. Draw one with both of us together, please."

Marudhanayagam nodded with a smile on his face. "Whatever the lady wants."

Jamie heard the indulgence in the man's voice and wondered for a brief moment if they had read the man wrong. He turned around to lift another stool and placed it next to the first one, inviting them to sit before pinning a fresh piece of canvas to the board in front of him. "You'll need to pay the cost in advance please," he said.

"We want to buy that painting of the bird too," said the MLA, pointing to the one his wife had been interested in.

"That'll be a total of Rs. 16,000, mate," said Jamie, turning to a young man seated behind him. "Can you please make a bill for the amount?"

Parthiban nodded, making the bill and receiving the cash, before Marudhanayagam sat next to his wife, holding her hand.

"I hope you wouldn't mind if I take a picture of the two of you. You know, sometimes certain angles turn even better on the camera and I use that for reference, only if necessary, of course." Jamie was glib with his excuse. He needed to send the man's picture to Vadivel and Shiva, like immediately.

The couple in front of him nodded their consent before Jamie quickly clicked a few shots on his iPhone. "Thank you. Please relax in your seats. This shouldn't take all that long." He quickly sketched Marudhanayagam and his wife in less than an hour and invited them to have a look at the result.

Sankari ooh'ed and aah'ed over the picture while Marudhanayagam didn't utter anything though deep down he was absolutely impressed. The artist had captured their likeness too perfectly.

"Do you have a facility to frame this?" asked Marudhanayagam. "We can hang it in our bedroom," he said, turning to his wife.

She smiled shyly before protesting. "No, no, let us hang it in the drawing room where everyone can see it."

The MLA nodded. "The wife is always right," he said, giving Jamie a sly wink.

Jamie gave him a smile which didn't quite reach his eyes before answering his earlier question. "You'll find a frame-maker further down, at stall no 23." Unpinning the canvas, he rolled it neatly and placed it in a circular cardboard container, screwing a lid over it before handing it to the MLA. Parthiban had already packed the framed painting of the bird and given the parcel to the lady. Jamie waved them off before sending the picture of the MLA and his wife to the *Keep Rhea Safe* WhatsApp group, adding the caption, "Target sighted, though with wife."

27

All of Jamie's paintings, except for two, were sold on the first day of the fair. And he had made twenty-one on-the-spot sketches in all. He shut his stall up at nine pm to go to High and Magic and have a drink there, watching the crowd swing to the DJ's tunes. The dance floor was packed with people, both young and old.

He sat on a tall stool at the bar, nursing his drink and watching the crowd. The last he knew, the politician had gone to have dinner at the Taj Mahal restaurant. Vadivel's man was keeping an eye out for him. Jamie planned to leave the premises only after he had confirmation that the MLA had left for the day. He wondered what the man meant to do now. Would he be back the next day? Marudhanayagam's wife's presence had thrown them all. Vadivel knew the man's background and was confident the MLA would never go near Rhea while his wife was with him.

The politician sat at the table for two, close to the wall at Taj Mahal, at the same time when Jamie was up at the disco, waiting for the maître d'hôtel to seat his wife on the chair opposite. As he ran his eyes down the menu, he saw Rhea Bansal entering the restaurant with a couple of guests. Marudhanayagam salivated, literally, his eyes running over her lissom body. His penchant for revenge took a backseat when he decided right at that moment, that he must have her, by hook or by crook. She must be as tall as he was, Marudhanayagam guessed, which was pretty tall for a woman. And her body was perfectly shaped, curved in the right places. He couldn't wait to get his hands on the twin globes which shook gently with each step she took.

"What?" Marudhanayagam turned to look at his wife with glazed eyes, not having heard a word of what she had been telling him. "I didn't hear you."

Sankari smiled at her husband. He was such a busy man and planned to run the country one day. She was so proud of him. He also had a lot of thinking and planning to do. Those were the times when she felt guilty whenever she said something which might distract him from his precious thoughts. And it seemed like it was one of those times now. "I wasn't saying anything important. You were busy thinking, I suppose," she said, with a deep respect in her voice.

Marudhanayagam nodded his head, without a qualm. "That's right. But it's alright. Today is all yours. So, tell me, what were you saying?"

Sankari looked at him adoringly. "Just that I want to have *seekh kabab* and *chicken biryani*. Would you like to share them with me?"

Her husband nodded with a smile on his face, surreptitiously noting that the managing director of the hotel was seated only a few tables away from them. In a way it was good she was facing the other way. He sighed. It was just that it was sad he could only view her back from where he was sitting.

Rhea spent the next half an hour chatting with Priya, her friend who owned the NGO, and her partner, Samsher, sharing a starter with them.

"The arrangements are simply amazing Rhea, even better than usual," said Priya, giving her friend a wide smile.

"And I think the artist's stall is a super hit. That Jamie Scott plays magic with his pencil," said Samsher. "You were lucky to get the man to participate in the fair."

Rhea kept the colour on her face from rising by sheer will power as she smiled first at Priya and then at Samsher, thanking them. "Even I'm impressed with the turn out. But I think the people have begun to see it as a regular event in Ooty nowadays. And my social media team has excelled itself with the promotions too."

"And it's just one day gone," said Priya, biting into the *achari paneer tikka* with relish.

"Fingers crossed," said Rhea, finishing her iced tea. "Will you guys excuse me, please? The stalls are winding up though the party will continue at the disco for those interested. Do feel free to check out the DJ. We are open till 1 am."

Samsher and Priya nodded as Rhea got up and left the restaurant from a side door.

When Marudhanayagam looked up from his half-eaten plate, he was disappointed to find that

Rhea wasn't sitting there with her guests, not any longer.

Well, no matter, he thought to himself as he gave a mental shrug. He planned to return the next day—alone. Ajit had his instructions and the MLA knew for a fact that the man was efficient.

Jamie spent a restless night, waking up a few times to check on Rhea, who slept undisturbed next to him. His gut told him the MLA was dangerous and would stoop to anything to get back at Rhea. While he was aware she was a Taekwondo black belt, he hadn't seen her in action, and hence wasn't all that confident. The plan was to catch the politician red-handed and for that they had to wait for the blow to strike.

Jamie's first instinct was to hold Rhea within the cocoon of his arms and not let any harm get to her, though he had no choice but to go with Vadivel's idea. That was the only way to net the slippery MLA. They had taken a number of precautions for this, even going so far as to having three CCTV cameras fitted in Rhea's office from different angles. Jamie had fixed the tiny electronic eyes—one to a painting of a rose which hung in her office, between two windows on her left, a second on the wall clock behind her chair and a third above the door. She wouldn't be able to locate any of them unless she actually looked for them. And he was ready to take the risk for Rhea's sake. They had to nail the man as soon as possible if Rhea was to lead a peaceful life. Marudhanayagam was a snake. Jamie only hoped she wouldn't kill Jamie after she got to know what he had got up to, bugging her office without her knowledge.

He hugged her close now, kissing her softly on her lips, half hoping she would wake up. His wish came true when Rhea smiled against his mouth, tracing its shape with the tip of her tongue, pressing her body close to his, her hand reaching down for his erection. "Make love to me?" she invited, pushing the comforter away. She traced a path with her lips all way to the pulse at his neck and brushed her tongue over it, excited when she felt it beating fast.

Jamie caressed her body with his large hands, his lips closing over the swollen tip of a breast, his tongue lazily rubbing against it. Rhea's whimpers excited him as he drew the nipple deep within his mouth, suckling hard.

Rhea explored his manhood with her hand, from the top to the tip, thrilled to feel him growing harder and bigger under her caress.

Transferring his mouth to her other breast, Jamie traced a path down her body with his hand, to find her feminine core, his fingers foraging deep within her wetness, stroking her steadily, as her muscles contracted with the build-up of an orgasm, only to stop a few seconds before she peaked.

"Jamie..." Rhea protested, "Why did you stop? I want you," she moaned, biting his shoulder.

Jamie grinned, his worry forgotten as he pushed her on the bed to climb over her, pulling both her legs around his waist. Without waiting any longer, he thrust his tumescent manhood into her eagerly awaiting vagina.

"Oh yes!" said Rhea, locking her legs at the ankles around his waist and throwing her arms around his strong back. She lifted her head to kiss Jamie on his lips, thrusting her tongue into his mouth, enthusiastically exploring the textures within. It wasn't long before she moaned long and loud as an orgasm hit her, shaking her to the core. She just knew she would never tire of having Jamie make love to her. She dug her nails hard into his smooth back as she felt him come within her a few seconds later, even as she exploded into another orgasm.

Jamie finally slept, his face buried against her breasts and her arms around him.

I t was four in the evening when Marudhanayagam was sighted at Rose Garden International on the second and final day of the Winter Fair. He was wearing the same suit and hat as the earlier day and by now Jamie, Shiva, Vadivel and his half a dozen sleuths could recognise him immediately.

Jamie was tense, his mind not really there when he hurriedly finished the sketch he was doing of a young woman, handing it over to Parthiban to pack. "Excuse me," he said, before leaving his stall vacant for a few brief moments to go check on Rhea from afar. A smile lit up his features when he saw her chatting with a guest who was checking out the Kanjeepuram silk saris and dress materials which were on display at one of the hotel's regular shops. He stood there for a few seconds watching her, not daring to go near her as he saw the MLA also eyeing her from four stalls away from the opposite side. Luckily, Jamie also noticed Vadivel's man standing not very far from the politician.

Jamie turned away abruptly and went back to his stall, though he wasn't sure if he could do any more sketches that day. He handed his visiting card—with a local SIM number written on the back—to a few disappointed prospective clients, apologising sweetly, pleading extreme tiredness. After all, he had already completed sixteen portrait sketches from morning. He could do with a drink as his throat felt parched. He turned to his Man Friday and requested him to go bring a couple of hot cappuccinos for the two of them. Too restless to sit, Jamie sipped from his takeaway cup, his eyes scanning the crowd, keeping track of the distance between Rhea and Marudhanayagam. He noticed that the man never went anywhere near her, though it was obvious—maybe only to Jamie—that he kept a watch on her from various angles.

It was past seven when Rhea turned to Ajit when she heard him say, "Ma'am," a trifle too loudly as he stood directly behind her.

"What?" she turned to the bellhop with a small scowl on her face. He was standing too close for her comfort. Shifting imperceptibly, she turned around to look at him directly, waiting for his answer.

"Shiva Sir wants you to go to your office immediately. He insisted it's urgent and sent me over to fetch you."

Rhea's frown deepened as she put her hand in her jacket pocket to reach for her walkie-talkie and realised why Shiva hadn't called and had sent Ajit Parmar with a message instead. Her walkie-talkie was missing. She dug into the pocket on the left and could still not find it. She wasn't aware that Ajit had taken the precaution to pick her pocket nimbly barely ten minutes ago. Not saying anything, she began to walk swiftly towards the main building, not really liking it when the bellhop followed her. He was probably getting back to his post at the reception, she presumed. What could be so urgent that Shiva wanted to see her? He knew she was busy. But then, Shiva was conscientious and would never call her unless it was something of an emergency.

Biting her lower lip, Rhea walked across the reception, nodding to Jasmine and Anand on her way towards the back and turned left to open the door to her office. She stepped in, pulling the door shut behind her, even as she spoke to the man sitting on one of the visitors' chairs. "What happened Shiva? Why did you...? You!" Her eyes went wide when she recognised the MLA as he turned around to leer at her. "What the hell are you doing in my office? Where's Shiva?" Black flames leaped out from her eyes as she glared furiously at the man who got up from his chair and began walking slowly towards her. She was too distracted to notice Ajit who had stepped in behind her and locked the door without a whisper of a noise.

"I don't care where Shiva is. You shouldn't either, Rhea Bansal," said Marudhanayagam, a lazy grin on his face as he ran his eyes from her chest to her narrow waist to her flaring hips down to her thighs.

Rhea felt calm stealing over her nerves as she centred herself quickly, breathing in and out steadily, clenching her hands loosely as she tucked them into the pockets of her jacket, getting ready to swing at the

MLA the moment he came too close. "What are you doing here in my office? Are you aware that you're trespassing?" she asked, her voice mild.

Marudhanayagam laughed, the sound grating on her nerves. "You do know I'm a powerful MLA, right? So, I'm trespassing. What do you plan to do about it? Why are we arguing, Rhea? Do you think I'm here to take revenge for your insult the other day? Not at all, my dear. You know what? I've been having sleepless nights thinking of you. I keep dreaming of your delicious and ripe body in my arms. You and I will make a great team. You are a shrewd businesswoman who's running this hotel so well. I am a powerful politician who plans to run this country one day. Don't you think we'll be explosive together?"

"It's your nose which is going to explode off your face if you come anywhere near me," said Rhea, not raising her voice by one decibel. No one seeing her would have known that her skin crawled at the MLA's words. She felt so dirty and besmirched by the thought that he had been thinking of her all these days, more like weeks. It was a wonder she didn't throw up on her office floor right this minute after hearing his words.

Marudhanayagam shrugged. "Well, if that's how you want it to be." He nodded to someone behind her, much to Rhea's shock. Worse was to come as she felt the iron band of an arm crushing against her chest before someone pulled both her hands to her back and tied them together at the wrists. Rhea tried kicking behind her, but the man kept dodging her even as his hands worked steadily.

"Good job, Ajit. You'll be well rewarded," said Marudhanayagam with a smirk on his face. "Do you think this is maybe a good time to co-operate, Rhea?"

Jamie's hands were clenched as he watched the computer screen where he could hear and see the politician, the bellhop and Rhea, from three different angles. He was all set to throttle the bastard. He knew Vadivel would ensure Ajit Parmar went to jail. But what if the sneaky slime-ball of a politician got away scot-free because of the clout he held?

He glared at the screen as the MLA continued to talk, "If you give in voluntarily, we can have a great time together. A woman with your kind of a body should be worshipped and let me tell you I'm the right man for it. I promise to give you the best fuck of your life," he said, leering lasciviously.

"Why don't you come closer?" said Rhea, tilting her head to eye him through the slit of her half-closed eyes.

"That's my girl," said Marudhanayagam, grinning widely, his teeth brilliantly white against his dark face. He walked one step closer and spoke to Ajit without taking his eyes off Rhea, "Get out, Ajit. I don't need you here anymore. And don't forget to lock the door behind you." He was confident he could deal with a mere woman. And if he needed to force himself on her, nothing could beat the pleasure.

Ajit Parmar was arrested the moment he stepped out of the room and clicked the lock behind him. He stared at the two hefty men as one of them clamped handcuffs on his wrists, while the other held a gun to his head, his jaw falling open in shock. "What? Who the hell are you?"

"Just shut up and go with us silently, unless you want to spend the rest of your life in jail," replied the policeman with the gun.

Ajit wasn't left with a choice but to obey when he saw Shiva standing there with his arms folded tightly across his chest, an angry expression on his face.

Vadivel placed a hand on Jamie's arm as the latter would have burst into Rhea's office. The police officer shook his head, raising two fingers in front of him. They could hear the muffled conversation between the two people within, now that they had moved closer to the door.

Marudhanayagam shoved a hand inside Rhea's unbuttoned jacket, placing a rough hand against her breast and squeezing hard, unable to control his excitement. Suddenly, the door flung open and Officer Vadivel rushed in with a gun in his hand. At the same instant, the MLA felt his right arm being wrenched and twisted behind him while his nose was punched hard. He was blinded for a moment before he shook his head to see a fuming, golden-haired giant standing in front of him, his eyes blazing green fire.

"How dare you?" choked Marudhanayagam, touching his swollen nose and shocked to see when his fingers came away with blood. "I'll have your passport cancelled."

Jamie laughed loudly, flexing his shoulders to remove the stress he had been under during the last few hours. "Go ahead and do your best," he challenged, shoving the politician away from him. He didn't really care if the man's arm was broken as he turned around to Rhea who stood rooted to her spot, absolutely shocked.

Vadivel removed a pair of handcuffs and locked them around the politician's wrists, only to have the MLA yell threateningly, "Don't you dare, Vadivel! You don't know the influence I wield. I'll get you for this."

Jamie cut through the knot on the rope tying Rhea's wrists and rubbed at the marks gently, pulling her against him.

"What the hell's going on?" she asked, her eyes wild as she looked up at his angry face.

Vadivel responded patiently to the MLA's threat. "I'm sure you will, sir. But right now, you're going to jail." He dragged the man away, saying, "I'll speak to you later, Jamie," and left with a wave of his hand.

Rhea wouldn't allow Jamie to kiss her when he tried. "Did you know something was going to happen?" she asked, a deep scowl on her face as she looked at him.

Jamie shrugged, giving a small nod.

"You are serious, right?" Rhea stared at him unbelievingly. "You mean you knew the man was going to try to rape me and you didn't bother to warn me about it!" She pinned him with her turbulent black gaze, valiantly pushing back the tears which sprang forth, her temper boiling out of control.

"I'm sorry, Rhea. There was no other way. I..."

Rhea backed away from him. "No other way? How dare you? How dare you run my life? Who the hell are you? Just because I slept with you doesn't make you my owner, Jamie Scott. I'll never tolerate this. No one gets away with trying to run my life." Rhea was screaming now; unlike the time she threatened the MLA in such a soft voice.

But her emotions hadn't been involved then. It looked like she had failed for the third time. And this time around, she had been so sure she had fallen for the right man. Her heart bled even as tears streamed down Rhea's face. This time, her feelings were for real. She was in love with Jamie Scott. But that still didn't mean she would allow him to take charge of her life. *If* they had got into a permanent relationship, it would have been as equal partners. But that was something which was never going to be. "Just get out of my life and stay out."

"Rhea, listen to me. I..." Jamie walked closer, only for her to raise a hand in front of her defensively.

"Just get out, Jamie, unless you want me to do something which we both might regret for life."

Jamie looked at the woman he had fallen in love with, desperately wanting to hold her close. But right now, she looked all set to murder him. Well, it wasn't as if he hadn't been expecting it. With a deep sigh, Jamie walked out of her office, shutting the door softly behind him, deciding to get sloshed. It was best to leave her alone until she calmed down. Or so he hoped!

Maybe, just maybe, he'll be able to make her see sense tomorrow morning. He was lucky to find an empty cottage for hire at Rose Garden International for the night when Jamie found out that Rhea had locked him out of her home. The next day, when he let himself into her cottage at eleven am—after realising she hadn't gone to work—he found the house was empty. Where the hell was Rhea?

He called Shiva who was to come on duty only at one pm. "Hello Shiva! Do you know where Rhea's gone?"

"Hello Jamie. Rhea ma'am has taken a break. I think the incident with the MLA was too much for her, on top of the hectic work prior to the fair. She has gone out of town."

"Do you know where?"

Shiva frowned. "No, she didn't tell me."

"Thanks, mate," said Jamie, disconnecting his cell phone. He tried calling Rhea a few times only to find her phone unreachable. She was probably travelling. With a deep sigh, Jamie had a shower and got ready for the day before going to meet Vadivel in his office.

Vadivel was looking grim. "Velusamy Nadar—Marudhanayagam's father-in-law—is sitting with the police commissioner as we talk. If the MLA gets out of this scot-free, I plan to quit the police force and that's a promise," he declared. Vadivel had made his feelings clear to his boss too.

"Are you saying all our efforts will go down the drain, just like that?" Jamie was shocked. Rhea had as good as dumped Jamie for his role in the fiasco. If the MLA got away after all this, then it would be too much of a bitter pill to swallow.

"Not if I have anything to do with it. Velusamy Nadar loves his daughter who is married to this lecher. All these years, the MLA had got away with everything because there was no proof. But now we have three sets of CCTV footages, which are more than enough to nail the man. Let's wait and see what Velusamy Nadar is trying to achieve."

Inside Police Commissioner Sakthivel's office, Velusamy Nadar was trying to strike a deal. There were just the two of them present. Velusamy knew fully well that Sakthivel could not be bought with money. So, he didn't even try to offer him a bribe. And then there was the fact that Velusamy was beyond angry with his son-in-law. The rascal had overreached himself this time. Velusamy had turned a blind eye to Marudhanayagam's exploits only because the latter had managed to slide out unscathed, each time. But this time round, the police had proof. And a 5-star hotelier wasn't exactly small fish. If this incident came out in the open, Sankari would be heartbroken. His innocent daughter had no clue of her husband's real character. Velusamy Nadar's hands trembled in a fine temper. He made a promise to Sakthivel which made the police commissioner's jaw drop. "I'll get the job done and send you the proof, I promise."

Seeing the fire in the older man's gaze, Sakthivel decided to let him have his way. A doctor arrived about half an hour later, sedating Marudhanayagam with an injection, not giving the MLA a chance to speak as Velusamy Nadar stood beside the doctor, supervising his actions. The MLA was taken away from the jailhouse attached to the commissioner's office on a stretcher and placed in an ambulance which carried him all the way to a private hospital in Coimbatore.

Marudhanayagam opened his eyes the next evening to find himself in a luxurious private room at the high-end hospital, his father-in-law dancing attention on him.

He smiled weakly at the older man, before laughing softly. "You are great, dear father-in-law. How did you ever manage to get me out of jail? Did you plead a heart condition or was it my liver?" he asked, his voice growing stronger with each word he uttered. The politician's energy had returned the moment he realised he was out of jail and Sankari's father was still at his side. He had been kind of worried the old man might disown him after his latest escapade. What he didn't realise was: Velusamy Nadar's love for his daughter was so powerful that he would go to any lengths to keep her husband safe, *for her sake* and for no other reason.

Velusamy Nadar stared, unsmiling, at his son-in-law who was lying on the hospital bed. "Rest easy, there won't be a cause for you to be arrested in the future either, at least not for molesting a woman," he responded in his guttural voice.

Marudhanayagam frowned. "I don't understand."

"I've had you surgically castrated. You won't be in a state to bed any woman, with or without her consent."

"Noooooo!" Marudhanayagam stared at his father-in-law in shock, but his voice came out only in a whisper as a sudden weakness assailed his body and mind. "How can you do this to your own daughter? Have you forgotten I am her husband?"

Velusamy's eyebrows went up to touch his pepper and salt hair. "I remember only too well you are my daughter's husband, a husband who hasn't been able to impregnate her—not in the twelve years of your marriage. Why do I care? This way, I have at least ensured you are kept safe from the law."

Of all the stupidest, moronic reasons! Marudhanayagam fumed in silence. "But I will have my revenge on Rhea Bansal. So what if she escaped from being raped? I will have her maimed or maybe even murdered," he declared, glaring at his father-in-law.

Velusamy laughed out loud. "And what about that Australian Jamie Scott? What do you plan to do with him?"

"I'll have his passport cancelled, have him put in jail for some terrible crime I'll frame him with. In fact, I'll have Rhea Bansal murdered and have it proven in court that Jamie Scott is the murderer." Marudhanayagam had an evil smile on his face as he smacked his lips, impressed with his own idea.

"You idiot!" Velusamy gave him a pitying look. "Do you know that Jamie Scott is a retired Interpol agent?"

Marudhanayagam shook his head. "You are wrong. That man is an artist, such an effeminate profession too," he said scornfully.

"Will you just shut up and listen to me? I know what I'm talking about. Scott retired early from Interpol because of an injury he suffered and has taken up a new career as an artist and interior designer. He has been helping Officer Vadivel gather evidence against you," snarled his father-in-law. "And Jamie Scott also happens to be Rhea Bansal's lover. You place a finger on her and you are a dead man. Always make your plans after you do your home-work right. Now listen to me! Here's my ultimatum to you! If you keep Sankari happy and play your politics right, in that order; while staying out of all shady deals, you will continue to have my complete support. I will help you run for the post of Chief Minister of Tamil Nadu. If I get to know—and believe me that I always do—you have been up to any kind of mischief, I'll have you kicked out of both, politics and your marriage. If you have any kind of imagination, I'm sure you will understand what that means. Do I make myself clear?" Velusamy gazed sternly at his son-in-law.

Marudhanayagam gave him a small nod, his expression bitter. The old man had made him impotent, literally and metaphorically.

29

J amie waited patiently for two days before trying to contact Rhea again, only to have her cut his call. Where must she have gone? He knew the Bansals were a close-knit family and stuck together despite the distances. He didn't know her parents well enough to casually call them and ask about their daughter. Rohit—Jamie shook his head to himself. Rhea's older brother will probably have his hide if he got to know Jamie had hurt his sister in any way. So that was out too. That left only Ritvik. Would Rhea's friendly younger brother tell him where she was? *Nothing ventured, nothing gained,* Jamie thought as he decided to call Ritvik.

Jamie dialled Ritvik's number and was startled when the line was disconnected immediately. He had not expected Rhea's family to turn against him. With a frown on his face, Jamie splashed colour on his canvas, his mind not really on what he was doing. How he missed her! His cell vibrated in his pocket, before stopping almost immediately. He took his phone out in a hurry to see it was a missed call from Ritvik Bansal. What the hell was he playing at?

Jamie called him back immediately. "Ritvik, is...?"

"Hey listen. I've got exactly twenty seconds before Rhea gets here. She's with me at my hotel, Maharaja International in Udaipur. Get the address from the internet and bring yourself here. She'll murder me if she gets to know I've been in touch with you. And *don't forget,*" Ritvik stressed the last two words, "I never called you. You called me. Got it?"

Jamie was grinning by now, not really bothered that the call was already cut. He packed his bag and booked a car to Coimbatore airport, planning to catch the first flight out to Udaipur. He reached the airport late at night to find out there was a flight at 7.55 am the next morning with a stopover in Mumbai for a couple of hours. Jamie bought the ticket as he didn't have a better option.

It had taken Rhea almost twelve hours to reach Udaipur. Ritvik took one look at her face and hugged her close. "Should I kill Jamie?" he offered, a tight look on his face. He had liked the Australian and felt bad that the man had hurt his precious sister.

Rhea shook her head. "If there's going to be a killing, I'll be doing it."

Phew! "What did he do?" He placed a cup of masala chai in her shaking hand—their mother's panacea for all ills.

Rhea sat back on the sofa at the suite Ritvik lived in at the hotel he owned and ran. "Ask me what he didn't do." She stirred the tea vigorously, not really aware of what she was doing as she stared down at her cup.

"What didn't he do?"

Rhea lifted her head and glared at Ritvik. "Jamie didn't tell me. He kept it a secret for I don't know how long. And why the hell did Officer Vadivel take Jamie into confidence? Men! They are all impossible," she declared.

Ritvik wondered where the conversation was going. Jamie had obviously done something to upset Rhea. No, he had *not* done something and that had upset Rhea. Who was Officer Vadivel? "Rhea, I think you'll need to tell me from the beginning. I can't understand a damn thing. What's the crime which Jamie has committed? I thought the guy was decent."

"So did I!" yelled Rhea, getting up to her feet, dumping her teacup on the centre table. "I thought he was decent too, unlike those others. But... but Ritvik," she howled, pressing her face to her brother's shoulder as he pulled her once again into his arms. "I trusted him Ritvik. He..."

"Did he cheat on you?" Ritvik all but snarled, suddenly looking way older, startling Rhea with the ferocity in his face and voice.

"Cheat? Jamie?" Rhea shook her head vigorously, "Of course not. Jamie's not the type to cheat. He's too honest and too much of a gentleman to cheat someone. He..."

Ritvik bit his lower lip to hide the smile which suddenly appeared on his face. "I did wonder if I had lost my touch at reading people correctly," he said with a straight face.

Rhea looked into his eyes keenly, not having missed the trace of mirth in his voice. "Are you laughing at me?" she growled.

"No, sis." Ritvik raised both hands in front of him in a gesture of defence. "Tell me what happened, from the beginning. I can't see where the conversation is going otherwise."

Rhea sighed, sitting down again to drink her tea. She told him what had happened in a few sentences, before concluding, "Jamie should have told me. He..."

"I'm sorry to interrupt. But if Jamie had told you before the event, they wouldn't have been able to catch the corrupt MLA red-handed, would they?" Ritvik asked her, his voice soft and gentle. He didn't want to upset his sister more than she already was.

"That's not the point, is it?"

"But that's the whole point, isn't it Rhea? If the man hadn't been caught with proof, he would have got away. He..."

"If Jamie had told me in advance, I'd have been more careful and ensured all safety precautions. I..."

"For how long? Throughout your life?" Ritvik asked her, a dark eyebrow up in query.

Rhea got up again. "I should have known you would side with Jamie. You men are all the same. You..."

"Come on Rhea. I never sided with Nayan; neither did Rohit nor Pappa. And we never thought well of

Sujit. It's not as if Jamie's right because he's a man. I can understand that you're upset. But look at it from his viewpoint. He..."

"I don't give a damn. Why should I? He could have consulted me about this before making his plan is what I think. Don't insist that I change my mind. Because I won't." She glared daggers at her brother.

Ritvik nodded. "Fine, have it your way," he shrugged, hugging her again. "I won't say a word, okay?"

Rhea calmed down a bit at that and said, "There's no need to say anything to Pappa, Mamma or Rohit, okay? Especially not Rohit. He's newly engaged and I don't want to upset him now. As far as they're concerned, I'm taking a break after the Winter Fair."

Ritvik nodded, grinning. "Okay sis, whatever you say."

Rhea couldn't stop an answering smile from appearing on her face. "And most importantly, don't you *dare* call Jamie and tell him I'm here. I want your promise on that."

"Are you sure?" Ritvik cocked an eyebrow at her, a mischievous look in his eyes.

"Ritvik! Promise me now."

He sighed dramatically, before placing his right palm against hers. "I promise."

Rhea had worn the carpet thin in Ritvik's living room over the two days she'd been there. Not one to remain idle, her mind was worse than a devil's workshop by now. Ritvik did his best to spend his free time with her, but he had a hotel to run too.

Jamie, Jamie, Jamie, Jamie—Rhea's mind went round and round the man she had fallen in love with; one she had trusted so completely. She did her best to hold on to her anger. But logic soon took over and she realised he might probably have been right in not telling her. But she was still curious as to why Officer Vadivel chose to take Jamie into his confidence.

She recalled the scene at her office. Rhea hadn't really been scared that day. She would have made mincemeat of the MLA even if she had to deal with him all by herself. But then, that would probably have made the man more vengeful. She sighed, wondering what must have happened to him now. Would he be in jail or had he already escaped using his power and influence?

And Jamie? What must he think of her? She had been terribly rude to a man who had treated her with so much love and care, one who had given her all the space she needed. He was the only man who knew how to let her be. And as for being her lover, he was simply adorable.

It was time to apologise. Rhea took her phone from her jeans pocket and speed-dialled Jamie's number before she changed her mind. She thought she imagined it when she could hear his phone ringing in both her ears. He took her call on the second ring and said, "Hey sweetheart!"

"Jamie, I'm sorry. I love you and I miss you terribly." Rhea told him in one breath.

The phone clicked in her ear as it disconnected, much to Rhea's shock. She whirled around when she continued to hear Jamie's voice. "I love you too, sweetheart." He was standing in the doorway, having dropped his backpack to the floor, his arms flung wide open. She ran into them, burying her face in his chest.

30

They were back in Ooty, at Rhea's home, the next day. She had organised a candlelight dinner, ordering some of their favourite Chinese dishes from the Noblesse restaurant. She wore a semi-transparent chiffon halter-necked dress, the colour of champagne, matched with pearls around her neck, wrists and in her ears. Her hair was piled into a loose knot and she looked exquisite to the man who walked into the living room, wearing a black tuxedo. Jamie whistled, giving her a wink, putting out a hand to take hers in it. He raised it to his lips, looking deeply into her eyes.

He was startled when Rhea suddenly went on her knees in front of him, holding his hand to her heart, saying, "Jamie, I love you. Will you marry me? I'll go to live in Australia with you if that's what you want."

"What?" Jamie gave her a surprised look. "Run that by me again?"

"Jamie. Can't you recognise a marriage proposal when you hear one? Will you put me out of my misery and say yes?" While she tried to appear completely confident, there was a tremor in Rhea's voice as she spoke the words.

Jamie continued to look at her, a mischievous glint in his jade eyes, a finger on his chin. "It's not a leap year. So how...?"

"Jamie!" Rhea jumped up to beat him on his chest with her tight fists.

He shook with laughter as he pulled her close. "Thank you, wild cat, I will."

Rhea threw her arms around his neck and kissed him hard, biting his thick lower lip. "Will you mind if I set up another 5-star hotel in Alice Springs? I would make a terrible housewife," she whispered in his ear, tracing the lobe with a damp tongue.

"Are you in a tearing hurry to settle down in Alice Springs?" asked Jamie, his forehead against hers as he stared into her dark gaze. "I was thinking of setting up shop in Ooty."

Rhea jumped up, locking her legs around his waist, totally excited. "Do you really mean that? Oh Jamie! That'll be just awesome."

He crushed her in his arms, kissing her deeply. "Yes, I do."

Jamie sat down on the sofa after dinner, holding Rhea in his lap. He pulled off a pearl earring from her lobe before tracing the shape of her ear with his tongue. "I think we are a perfect pair—a high powered business woman and a laidback artist. What say?" He grinned, kissing her soft cheek.

Rhea moved a couple of inches away to look up at his face. "And what is the Interpol agent's role in all this?" she asked, her eyes turning serious.

"Nothing." Jamie shrugged. "You know I'm an ex-agent."

"Why did you quit?" Rhea was curious. "Not that I mind. I don't think you'd have ever come down to Ooty with your high-flying career."

"There was a reason for it. I got shot during action in Mexico a couple of years ago. My thigh bone shattered and I had to undergo multiple surgeries. I was stuck to a wheelchair for more than six months. The doctors weren't confident I'd walk normally ever again..."

Rhea stared at him in horror, both her hands over her mouth. "Oh my God! Does it still hurt?" She jumped off his lap, worried she might be making it worse for him.

Jamie laughed as he pulled her right back into his lap. "Not any more. I never believed what the doctors said. I just *knew* I'd be back to normal. And so, here I am," he grinned. "As for coming over to Ooty, it had always been there at the back of my mind. But the time needed to be right, I suppose. The aborigines would say *it's the call of the soul*. If I had come here before Rose Garden International, I'd have probably never met you. And since our getting together was meant to be..." Jamie grinned at her. "Everything happens at the exact right time."

Jamie recalled the words from his grandmother's missing diary which he had found in Rhea's home...

June 6, 1945
Dear Diary,

Nathan was born to us two days ago—a squirming bundle of joy, a gift from heaven. Jason is on top of the world and planning our baby's future already, building a cricket pitch in our backyard. He has even booked a foal which will be born in six months or so. I am so happy and blessed. Am I glad we decided to move to Ooty! The tranquillity of the place has brought such love and joy into our lives. While Ooty is paradise, Rose Garden is Home Sweet Home.

Well, I need to go. Nathan wants his feed. Until tomorrow,

Yours sincerely,
Barbara

And just like they had for Barbara and Jason, Ooty and Rose Garden International had brought love and joy into Jamie and Rhea's lives too!

THE END

BIBLIOGRAPHY

- *Organisational Behaviour in Hotels and Restaurants - An International Perspective* by Yvonne Guerrier.
- *Food and Beverage Service* - 5th edition by Dennis Lillicrap, John Cousins and Robert Smith.
- *The Catering Management HAND BOOK* (The Complete Guide to Hotel, Restaurant and outside catering) Edited by Judy Ridgway, Brian Ridgway
- *Effective Purchase Practices for Hotels and Restaurants in India* – F H & R A INDIA (November, 2003)
- *Guidelines and Incentives for Hotel Industry in India* – F H & R A INDIA (November, 2003)
- *Foods that Harm, Foods that Heal* – Published by Reader's Digest Association Limited

MORE BOOKS
BY
SUNDARI
VENKATRAMAN

SUNDARI
VENKATRAMAN
AMAZON BESTSELLING AUTHOR
THE BANSAL LEGACY
BOOK #1
SIMHA
INTERNATIONAL

SIMHA INTERNATIONAL
(The Bansal Legacy #1)

Rohit Bansal, the handsome and suave managing director of Simha International, is the envy of many—from a director of the hotel to an employee.

A thief comes up with a simple modus operandi, believing that nobody's really going to find out anything about the thefts taking place. But when a guest brings it to his notice, Rohit is determined to save the reputation of Simha International and ropes in a top-notch detective. Will Rohit be able to find who the thief is before time runs out?

The lovely and intelligent Tasha Sawant goes to work at Simha International as the duty manager. Her experience in the hotel industry only adds to the hotel's excellent service.

Tasha is attracted to Rohit and it would seem that he reciprocates her feelings. Well, the lady isn't looking for a permanent relationship as it looks like she has already had an unpleasant experience. But then, what about the guy? Does Rohit want any kind of relationship with Tasha?

Simha International is the first book in The Bansal Legacy trilogy

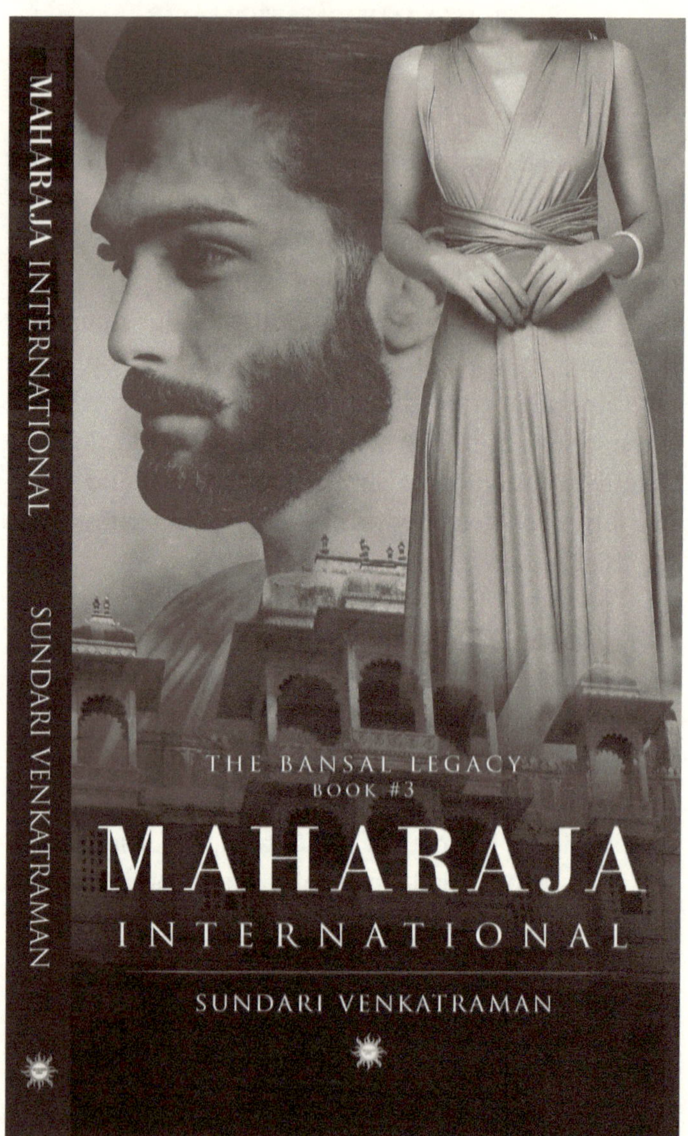
MAHARAJA INTERNATIONAL
SUNDARI VENKATRAMAN
THE BANSAL LEGACY
BOOK #3
MAHARAJA
INTERNATIONAL
SUNDARI VENKATRAMAN

MAHARAJA INTERNATIONAL
(The Bansal Legacy #3)

Ritvik Bansal's decision to father a surrogate child comes as a total shock to his family, more because he insists that he needs no wife.

Two years down the line, Sia Rathod goes to work at Ritvik's 5-star hotel Maharaja International as the salon manager at Cleopatra's.

They connect instantaneously as sparks fly. After spending time in each other's company, they take their relationship to the next level.

Will Ritvik change his mind about getting married?

Even if he does, will Sia agree to become his wife as well as to be mother to two-year-old Aarya? Especially with the kind of past which she never speaks about?

**Maharaja International* is the third and last book in The Bansal Legacy trilogy

Mr. Perfect
SUNDARI VENKATRAMAN

MR. PERFECT

Saloni Malhotra is miserable with her lonely and servile existence in Chicago, while her husband Dr Manish Chawla is too selfish to be bothered about his wife's happiness. It's watching her sister's closeness to her new husband that actually opens Saloni's eyes to the lack in her life.

Aarav Chopra hasn't looked at another woman since he fell in love with the seventeen-year-old Saloni. The nine years in-between seem to disappear when he sets eyes on her again at her sister's wedding. But this time round, his love stretches to include her son too, as Mitesh holds not just Aarav's finger but also his heart in his little hand.

Things come to a head when she flees Chicago to return to Delhi along with her baby son Mitesh.

Life throws Saloni and Aarav together as she goes to work in his group of companies while awaiting her divorce. The attraction is as powerful as ever! But Saloni is absolutely clear that she wouldn't be tied to a man ever again.

Will Aarav be able to convince her otherwise?

Connect with Sundari Venkatraman here:

Sundari Venkatraman Books

Sundari Venkatraman Books

https://www.sundarivenkatraman.in

Author Sundari Venkatraman

@sundarivenkat

@sundarivenkatraman

sundarivenkat@gmail.com